WILDFIRE AT LARCH CREEK

A FIREHAWKS SMOKEJUMPER ROMANCE

M. L. BUCHMAN

Buchman Bookworks

SIGN UP FOR M. L. BUCHMAN'S NEWSLETTER TODAY

and receive:
Release News
Free Short Stories
a Free Novel

Do it today. Do it now.
www.mlbuchman.com/newsletter

Other works by M. L. Buchman:

CHAPTER 1

wo-Tall Tim Harada leaned over Akbar the Great's shoulder to look out the rear door of the DC-3 airplane.

"Ugly," he shouted over the roar of the engine and wind.

Akbar nodded rather than trying to speak.

Since ugly was their day job, it didn't bother Tim much, but this was worse than usual. It would be their fourth smokejump in nine days on the same fire. The Cottonwood Peak Fire was being a total pain in the butt, even worse than usual for a wildfire. Every time they blocked it in one direction, the swirling winds would turnabout and drive the fire toward a new point on the compass. Typical for the Siskiyou Mountains of northern California, but still a pain.

Akbar tossed out a pair of crepe paper streamers and they watched together. The foot-wide streamers caught wind and curled, loop-the-looped through vortices, and reversed direction at least three times. Pretty much the worst conditions possible for a parachute jump.

"It's what we live for!"

Akbar nodded and Tim didn't have to see his best friend's face to know about the fierce wildness of his white grin on his Indian-dark face. Or the matching one against his own part-Vietnamese coloring. Many women told him that his mixed Viet, French-Canadian, and

1

Oklahoman blood made him intriguingly exotic—a fact that had never hurt his prospects in the bar.

The two of them were the first-stick smokejumpers for Mount Hood Aviation, the best freelance firefighters of them all. This was—however moronic—*precisely* what they lived for. He'd followed Akbar the Great's lead for five years and the two of them had climbed right to the top.

"Race you," Akbar shouted then got on the radio and called directions about the best line of attack to "DC"—who earned his nickname from his initials matching the DC-3 jump plane he piloted.

Tim moved to give the deployment plan to the other five sticks still waiting on their seats; no need to double check it with Akbar, the best approach was obvious. Heck, this was the top crew. The other smokies barely needed the briefing; they'd all been watching through their windows as the streamers cavorted in the chaotic winds.

Then, while DC turned to pass back over the jump zone, he and Akbar checked each others' gear. Hard hat with heavy mesh face shield, Nomex fire suit tight at the throat, cinched at the waist, and tucked in the boots. Parachute and reserve properly buckled, with the static line clipped to the wire above the DC-3's jump door. Pulaski fire axe, fire shelter, personal gear bag, chain saw on a long rope tether, gas can...the list went on, and through long practice took them under ten seconds to verify.

Five years they'd been jumping together, the last two as lead stick. Tim's body ached, his head swam with fatigue, and he was already hungry though they'd just eaten a full meal at base camp and a couple energy bars on the short flight back to the fire. All the symptoms were typical for a long fire.

DC called them on close approach. Once more Akbar leaned out the door, staying low enough for Tim to lean out over him. Not too tough as Akbar was a total shrimp and Tim had earned the "Two-Tall" nickname for being two Akbars tall. He wasn't called Akbar the Great for his height, but rather for his powerful build and unstoppable energy on the fire line.

"Let's get it done and..." Tim shouted in Akbar's ear as they approached the jump point.

"...come home to Mama!" and Akbar was gone.

Tim actually hesitated before launching himself after Akbar and ended up a hundred yards behind him.

Come home to Mama? Akbar had always finished the line, *Go get the girls.* Ever since the wedding, Akbar had gotten all weird in the head. Just because he was married and happy was no excuse to—

The static line yanked his chute. He dropped below the tail of the DC-3—always felt as if he had to duck, but doorways on the ground did the same thing to him—and the chute caught air and jerked him hard in the groin.

The smoke washed across the sky. High, thin cirrus clouds promised an incoming weather change, but wasn't going to help them much today. The sun was still pounding the wilderness below with a scorching, desiccating heat that turned trees into firebrands at a single spark.

The Cottonwood Peak Fire was chewing across some hellacious terrain. Hillsides so steep that some places you needed moun- taineering gear to go chase the flames. Hundred-and-fifty foot Doug firs popping off like fireworks. Ninety-six thousand acres, seventy percent contained and a fire as angry as could be that they were beating it down.

Tim yanked on the parachute's control lines as the winds caught him and tried to fling him back upward into the sky. On a jump like this you spent as much time making sure that the chute didn't tangle with itself in the chaotic winds as you did trying to land somewhere reasonable.

Akbar had called it right though. They had to hit high on this ridge and hold it. If not, that uncontained thirty percent of the wildfire was going to light up a whole new valley to the east and the residents of Hornbrook, California were going to have a really bad day.

His chute spun him around to face west toward the heart of the blaze. Whoever had rated this as seventy percent contained clearly needed his head examined. Whole hillsides were still alight with flame. It was only because the MHA smokies had cut so many fire-breaks over the last eight days, combined with the constant pounding of the big Firehawk helicopters dumping retardant loads every which way, that the whole mountain range wasn't on fire.

Tim spotted Akbar. Below and to the north. Damn but that guy could fly a chute. Tim dove hard after him.

Come home to Mama! Yeesh! But the dog had also found the perfect lady. Laura Jenson: wilderness guide, expert horsewoman—who was still trying to get Tim up on one of her beasts—and who was really good for Akbar. But it was as if Tim no longer recognized his best friend.

They used to crawl out of a fire, sack out in the bunks for sixteen-straight, then go hit the bars. *What do I do for a living? I parachute out of airplanes to fight wildfires by hand.* It wowed the women every time, gained them pick of the crop.

Now when Akbar hit the ground, Laura would be waiting in her truck and they'd disappear to her little cabin in the woods. What was up with that anyway?

Tim looked down and cursed. He should have been paying more attention. Akbar was headed right into the center of the only decent clearing, and Tim was on the verge of overflying the ridge and landing in the next county.

He yanked hard on the right control of his chute, swung in a wide arc, and prayed that the wind gods would be favorable just this once. They were, by inches. Instead of smacking face first into the drooping top of a hemlock that he hadn't seen coming, he swirled around it, receiving only a breath-stealing slap to the ribs, and dropped in close beside Akbar.

"Akbar the Great rules!"

His friend demanded a high five for making a cleaner landing than Tim's before he began stuffing away his chute.

In two minutes, the chutes were in their stuff bags and they'd shifted over to firefighting mode. The next two sticks dropped into the space they'd just vacated. Krista nailed her landing more cleanly than Tim or Akbar had. Jackson ate an aspen, but it was only a little one, so he was on the ground just fine, but he had to cut down the tree to recover his chute. Didn't matter; they had to clear the whole ridge anyway—except everyone now had an excuse to tease him.

FORTY HOURS later Tim had spent thirty hours non-stop on the line and ten crashed face first into his bunk. Those first thirty had been a grueling battle of clearing the ridgeline and scraping the earth down to mineral soils. The heat had been obscene as the fire climbed the face of the ridge, rising until it had towered over them in a wall of raging orange and thick, smoke-swirl black a couple dozen stories high.

The glossy black-and-racing-flame painted dots of the MHA Firehawks had looked insignificant as they dove, dropping eight tons of bright-red retardant alongside the fire or a thousand gallons of water directly on the flames as called for. The smaller MD500s were on near-continuous call-up to douse hotspots where sparks had jumped the line. Emily, Jeannie, and Vern, their three night-drop certified pilots, had flown right through the night to help them kill it. Mickey and the others picking it back up at daybreak.

Twice they'd been within minutes of having to run and once they were within seconds of deploying their fire shelters, but they'd managed to beat it back each time. There was a reason that smoke-jumpers were called on a Type I wildfire incident. They delivered. And the Mount Hood Aviation smokies had a reputation of being the best in the business; they'd delivered on that as well.

Tim had hammered face down into his bunk, too damn exhausted to shower first. Which meant his sheets were now char-smeared and he'd have to do a load of laundry. He jumped down out of the top bunk, shifting sideways to not land on Akbar if he swung out of the lower bunk at the same moment...except he wasn't there. His sheets were neat and clean, the blanket tucked in. Tim's were the only set of boots on the tiny bit of floor the two of them usually jostled for.

Akbar now stayed overnight in the bunkhouse only if Laura was out on a wilderness tour ride with her horses.

Tim thought about swapping his sheets for Akbar's clean ones, but it hardly seemed worth the effort.

Following tradition, Tim went down the hall, kicking the doors and receiving back curses from the crashed-out smokies. The MHA base camp had been a summer camp for Boy Scouts or something way too many years ago. The halls were narrow and the doors thin.

"Doghouse!" he hollered as he went. He raised a fist to pound on Krista's door when a voice shouted from behind it.

"You do that, Harada, and I'm gonna squish your tall ass down to Akbar's runt size."

That was of course a challenge and he beat on her door with a quick rattle of both fists before sprinting for the safety of the men's showers.

Relative safety.

He was all soaped up in the doorless plywood shower stall, when a bucket of ice-cold water blasted him back against the wall.

He yelped! He couldn't help himself. She must have dipped it from the glacier-fed stream that ran behind the camp it was so freaking cold.

Her raucous laugh said that maybe she had.

He considered that turnabout might be fair play, but with Krista you never knew. If he hooked up a one-and-a-half inch fire hose, she might get even with a three hundred-gallon helicopter drop. And then... Maybe he'd just shame her into buying the first round at the Doghouse Inn.

Tim resoaped and scrubbed and knew he'd still missed some patches of black. The steel sheets attached to the wall as mirrors were as useless now as they'd been before decades of Boy Scouts had tried to carve their initials into them. Usually he and Akbar checked each other because you ended up with smoke or char stains in the strangest spots.

But Akbar wasn't here.

Tim didn't dare wait for any of the others. If he was caught still in the shower by all the folks he'd just rousted from their sacks, it wouldn't turn out well.

He made it back to his room in one piece. The guys who'd showered last night were already on their way out. Good, they'd grab the table before he got down into town and hit the Doghouse Inn. The grimy ones weren't moving very fast yet.

Tim had slept through breakfast and after the extreme workout of a long fire his stomach was being pretty grouchy about that.

CHAPTER 2

a *s Macy Tyler prepared* for it, she regretted saying yes to a date
with Brett Harrison. She regretted not breaking the date the
second after she'd made it. And she hoped that by the time the
evening with Brett Harrison was over she wouldn't regret not dying
of some exotic Peruvian parrot flu earlier in the day.

Just because they'd both lived in Larch Creek, Alaska their entire
lives was not reason enough for her to totally come apart. Was it?

Actually it was nothing against Brett particularly. But she knew
she was still borderline psychotic about men. It was her first date
since punching out her fiancé on the altar, and the intervening six
months had not been sufficient for her to be completely rational on
the subject.

After fussing for fifteen minutes, she gave herself up as a lost
cause. Macy hanked her dark, dead straight, can't-do-crap-with-it
hair back in a long ponytail, put on a bra just because—it was mostly
optional with her build, and pulled on a t-shirt. Headed for the door,
she caught sight of herself in the hall mirror and saw which t-shirt
she'd grabbed: *Helicopter Pilots Get It Up Faster.*

She raced back to her bedroom and switched it out for: *People Fly
Airplanes, Pilots Fly Helicopters.* And knocked apart her ponytail in the

process. Hearing Brett's pickup on the gravel street, she left her hair down, grabbed a denim jacket, and headed for the door.

Macy hurried out and didn't give Brett time to climb down and open the door of his rattletrap Ford truck for her, if he'd even thought of it.

"Look nice, Macy," was all the greeting he managed which made her feel a little better about the state of her own nerves.

He drove into town, which was actually a bit ridiculous, but he'd insisted he would pick her up. Town was four blocks long and she only lived six blocks from the center of it. They rolled down Buck Street, up Spitz Lane, and down Dave Court to Jack London Avenue—which had the grandest name but was only two blocks long because of a washout at one end and the back of the pharmacy-gas station at the other.

This north side of town was simply "The Call" because all of the streets were named for characters from *The Call of the Wild*. French Pete and Jack London had sailed the Alaskan seaways together. So, as streets were added, the founders had made sure they were named after various of London's books. Those who lived in "The Fang" to the south were stuck with characters from *White Fang* for their addresses including: Grey Beaver Boulevard, Weedon Way, and Lip-lip Lane.

Macy wished that she and French Pete's mate Hilma—he went on to marry an Englishwoman long after he'd left and probably forgotten Larch Creek—hadn't been separated by a century of time; the woman must have really been something.

Macy tried to start a conversation with Brett, but rapidly discovered that she'd forgotten to bring her brain along on this date and couldn't think of a thing to say.

They hit the main street at the foot of Hal's Folly—the street was only the length of the gas station, named for the idiot who drove a dogsled over thin ice and died for it in London's book. It was pure irony that the street was short and steep. When it was icy, the Folly could send you shooting across the town's main street and off into Larch Creek—which was much more of a river than a creek. The street froze in early October, but the river was active enough that you didn't want to go skidding out onto the ice before mid-November.

Brett drove them up past the contradictory storefronts which were all on the "high side" of the road—the "low side" and occasionally the road itself disappeared for a time during the spring floods. The problem was that almost all of the buildings were from the turn of the century, but half were from the turn of this century and half were from the turn before. The town had languished during the 1900s and only experienced a rebirth over the last four decades.

Old log cabins and modern stick-framed buildings with generous windows stood side by side. Mason's Galleria was an ultramodern building of oddly-shaded glass and no right angles. One of the town mysteries was how Mason kept the art gallery in business when Larch Creek attracted so few tourists. Macy's favorite suggestion was that the woman—who was always dressed in the sharpest New York clothes and spoke so fast that no one could understand her—was actually a front for the Alaskan mafia come to rule Larch Creek.

This newest, most modern building in town was tight beside the oldest and darkest structure.

French Pete's, where Brett parked his truck, was the anchor at the center of town and glowered out at all of the other structures. The heavy-log, two-story building dominated Parisian Way—as the main street of Larch Creek was named by the crazy French prospector who founded the town in the late-1800s. He'd named the trading post after himself and the town after the distinctive trees that painted the surrounding hills yellow every fall. French Pete had moved on, but a Tlingit woman he'd brought with him stayed and bore him a son after his departure. It was Hilma who had made sure the town thrived.

There had been a recent upstart movement to rename the town because having the town of Larch Creek *on* Larch Creek kept confusing things. "Rive Gauche" was the current favorite during heavy drinking at French Pete's because the town was on the "left bank" of Larch Creek. If you were driving in on the only road, the whole town was on the left bank; like the heart of Paris. The change had never made it past the drinking stage, so most folk just ignored the whole topic, but it persisted on late Saturday nights.

Macy took strength from the town. She had loved it since her first memories. And just because she'd been dumb enough to agree to a date with Brett, she wasn't going to blame Larch Creek for that.

Well, not much. Perhaps, if there were more than five hundred folk this side of Liga Pass, there would be a single man that she could date who didn't know every detail of her life. She still clung onto the idea that she'd find a decent man somewhere among the chaff.

Dreamer!

That wasn't entirely fair. After all, some of them, like Brett, were decent enough.

The problem was that she, in turn, knew every detail of their lives. Macy had gone to school with each of them for too many years and knew them all too well. A lot of her classmates left at a dead run after graduation and were now up in Fairbanks, though very few went further afield. The thirty-mile trip back to Larch Creek from "the city" might as well be three hundred for how often they visited. The first half of the trip was on Interstate 4 which was kept open year round. But once you left the main highway, the road narrowed and twisted ten miles over Liga Pass with harsh hairpins and little forgiveness. It didn't help that it was closed as often as it was open in the winter months. The last five miles were through the valley's broad bottom land.

The town was four blocks long from the Unitarian church, which was still a movie theater on Friday and Saturday nights, at the north end of town to the grange at the south end. The houses crawled up the hills to the east. And the west side of the fast-running, glacier-fed river, where the forested hills rose in an abrupt escarpment, belonged to bear, elk, and wolf. Only Old Man Parker had a place on that side, unable to cross during fall freeze-up or spring melt-out. But he and his girlfriend didn't come into town much even when the way was open across running water or thick ice.

The main road ran north to meet the highway to Fairbanks, and in the other direction ended five miles south at Tena. Tena simply meant "trail" in the Tanana dialect and added another couple dozen families to the area. The foot trail out of Tena lead straight toward the massif of Denali's twenty-thousand foot peak which made the valley into a picture postcard.

Macy did her best to draw strength from the valley and mountain during the short drive to French Pete's. Once they hit Parisian Way, a bit of her brain returned. She even managed a polite inquiry about Brett's construction business and was pretty pleased at having done so. Thankfully they were close, so his answer was kept brief.

"Mostly it's about shoring up people's homes before winter hits. There are only a couple new homes a year and Danny gets most of those." He sounded bitter, it was a rivalry that went back to the senior prom and Cheryl Dahl, the prettiest Tanana girl in town.

The fact that Brett and Danny drank together most Saturdays and Cheryl had married Mike Nichol—the one she'd accompanied to the prom—and had three equally beautiful children in Anchorage had done nothing to ease their epic rivalry.

Or perhaps it was because Brett's blue pickup had a bumper sticker that said *America Is Under Construction* and Danny's blue truck had a drawing of his blue bulldozer that read *Vogon Constructor Fleet— specialist in BIG jobs.*

"Small towns," Macy said in the best sympathetic tone she could muster. It was difficult to not laugh in his face, because it was *so* small-town of them.

"This place looks wackier every time," they'd stopped in front of French Pete's. "Carl has definitely changed something, just can't pick it out."

Macy looked up in surprise. The combined bar and restaurant appeared no different to her. Big dark logs made a structure two-stories high with a steep roof to shed the snow. A half dozen broad steps led up to a deep porch that had no room for humans; it was jammed with Carl Deville's collection of "stuff."

"Your junk. My stuff," Carl would always say when teased about it by some unwary tourist. After such an unthinking comment, they were then as likely to find horseradish in their turkey sandwich as not.

There was the broken Iditarod sled from Vic Hornbeck's failed race bid in the late 1970s piled high with dropped elk antlers. An Elks Lodge hat from Poughkeepsie, New York still hung over one handle of the sled. The vintage motorcycle of the guy who had come through on his way to solo climb up Denali from the north along Muldrow Glacier and descend to the south by Cassin Ridge was still there, buried under eleven years of detritus. Whether he made the crossing and didn't come back or died on the mountain, no one ever knew.

"Man asked me to hold it for him a bit," Carl would offer in his deep laconic style when asked by some local teen who lusted after the wheels. "Don't see no need to hustle it out from under him. 'Sides, the baby girl he left in Carol Swenson's belly whilst he was here is ten now. Mayhaps she'll want it at sixteen."

There was an old wooden lobster pot—that Macy had never understood because the Gulf of Alaska to the south wasn't all that much closer than the Beaufort Sea to the north and the pot looked like it was from Maine—with a garden gnome-sized bare-breasted hula dancer standing inside it; her ceramic paint worn to a patina by too many Alaskan winters spent topless and out of doors. A hundred other objects were scattered about including worn-out gold panning equipment, a couple of plastic river kayaks with "For Rent" signs that might have once been green and sky blue before the sun leached out all color—though she'd never seen them move. And propped in the corner was the wooden propeller from Macy's first plane that she'd snapped when her wheel had caught in an early hole in the permafrost up near Nenana. That was before she'd switched to helicopters. She'd spent a week there before someone could fly in a replacement.

"Looks the same to me."

Brett eyed her strangely as he held open the door.

And just like that she knew she'd blown what little hope this date had right out of the water. Brett had been trying to make conversation and she'd done her true-false test. It wasn't like she was anal, it was more like everyone simply treated her as if she was.

Inside was dark, warm, and just as cluttered. A century or more of oddbits had been tacked to the walls: old photos, snowshoes strung with elk hide, a rusted circular blade several feet across from the old sawmill that had closed back in the sixties, and endless other bits and pieces that Carl and his predecessors had gathered. He claimed direct lineage back to French Pete Deville, through Hilma. It wasn't hard to believe; Carl looked like he'd been born behind the bar. Looked like he might die there too.

The fiction section of the town library lined one long wall of French Pete's. Most of the non-fiction was down at the general store except for religion, movies, and anything to do with mechanics. They were down in the movie house-church's lobby, the mechanical guides because the pharmacy-gas station was next door.

Though Carl didn't have any kin, Natalie, the ten-year-old daughter of Carol Swenson and the mountain climber with the left-behind motorcycle, was sitting up on a high barstool playing chess against Carl. It was a place she could be found most days when there wasn't school and Carol was busy over at the general store and post office. She was such a fixture that over the last few years everyone had pretty much come to expect Natty to take over French Pete's someday.

Macy scanned the tables hoping that no one would recognize her, fat chance in a community the size of Larch Creek.

And then she spotted the big table back in the corner beneath the moose-antler chandelier. It was packed.

Oh crap! She'd forgotten it was Sunday.

Too late to run for cover, she guided Brett in the other direction to a table in the corner. She managed to sit with her back to her father's expression of mock horror. That she could deal with.

But it would have been easier if Mom hadn't offered a smile and a wink.

His GUT now rumbling in anticipation of at least getting brunch,

Tim drove down off the mountain from the high camp used by Mount Hood Aviation. It was a gray, drizzling July day. The kind that promised no new fires. It was the first good soaking the forests had received in months, but it wasn't ripping through in some violent whorl of thunder and a storm of lightning to kick off another fifty fires. Just a slow Pacific Northwest drizzle, warm and muggy.

As he drove down the winding road toward the town of Hood River, he remembered when such days had chaffed at him. As a rookie smokejumper all he cared about was that he was only paid when he was on the jump. No fires meant no money which meant fewer cool toys.

Five years up in the mountains and the remote wilderness had taught him about the hell that the landscape paid, and the people. Steve Mercer, MHA's drone pilot, would never walk right again because of an accident as a smokie. Tim had lost both friends and mentors in the jump and in the fire. He'd lost five to a vehicle accident one year; a wilderness tanker truck bringing out a team after they'd beaten the fire, had swung wide on a back logging road. The sodden shoulder had given away and they'd rolled all the way down the high bank into the Rogue River. Anyone that survived the roll had drowned trapped in the vehicle.

If Mother Nature wanted to give Tim a rain break, he'd take it happily. Not that he'd ever let another smokie know that, not even Akbar. He had his pride after all.

The Doghouse Inn was packed. The soft rain had also chased all of the windsurfers out of the Columbia Gorge. So even though it was more brunch than lunchtime, the place was thick with immensely fit young women in tight t-shirts and shorts. There were men too, but playing the smokejumper card always trumped anything they could bring to the table, so they didn't count.

"Tim!" Amy came out from behind the bar and laid on one of her hugs. Damn but women weren't supposed to feel that good, especially when they were married to the cook who had fists the size of bowling balls.

"Hey beautiful!" he did the catch-and-release thing, but still felt better for it. Shot a wave to Gerald in the back.

The guys were at the central table: Mickey, Gordon, and Vern, the pilots of the small MD500 helicopters. Mickey waved him over, but the open seat by Vern had better positioning on a group of hot windsurfers.

Then he spotted Akbar and Laura off to the side at a small table against the wall; he just had to go over and give them shit for doing the "couple" thing. He took the ice tea Amy held out for him, signaled for Vern to hold the seat next to him, and headed for Akbar.

"Akbar the Great, holding hands in public. Never thought I'd see the day," Tim hooked over a chair and sat down at the table partway into the aisle. That left him facing the giant Snoopy World War I fighting ace painted on the wood-paneled wall. The entire interior of the Doghouse was covered floor to ceiling with photos of dogs and their crazy doghouses, except the one wall where Snoopy dominated the landscape in his never ending battle with the Red Baron.

Akbar raised his hand, which lifted Laura's as well, "Yeah, who'd have thought."

"Ruined a perfectly good bachelor there, Laura." Tim was looking for some good tease but the two of them just ate it up. He'd been best man at their wedding and it still struck him as plenty strange.

"Proud to have. Of course I hadn't pictured falling for an arrogant, full-of-himself smokejumper."

"I'm only arrogant if I don't live up to my reputation."

Laura ignored her husband, "I always pictured some nice, sophisticated quiet type like...you." She spoiled her tease with a delightful giggle.

"Ah, if I'd met you first, lady—"

She shook her head, "Too much of a good thing, Tim. I'd have overdosed. I settled for Akbar and that has worked out just fine for me."

Tim drank back a large hit of his ice tea, but his throat felt no less dry for it. If only he didn't like Laura, it would be easier. But he'd put his seal of approval on her way back when the two of them were first dating and she'd never given him a single reason to take it back. They were amazing together. But the thing was, they were just…together.

And he was sitting here being a third wheel.

"Did you hear that we're supposed to get rain for a week?" Akbar kept Tim in his seat a moment longer.

Tim hadn't.

"Henderson said we're going dark. A whole week off in July, how's that for a crazy-ass thing? Even the Bureau of Land Management smoke teams are being pulled off the remaining fires because the rains are doing their work for them. We freelancers are totally off the hook for seven days…as long as we keep our phones with us of course."

"Of course," Tim echoed. A week off. He looked over his shoulder at the guys playing the game. Not a single woman there was a week-off sort. These were one night stands or hot-and-heavy weekend flings. And there were definitely no Laura Jensons there; not a one.

A week?

Normally he could fill a week with a whole string of hot women, but sitting here with Akbar and Laura, it didn't feel so tempting.

He turned back to them and tried to slide into his usual form.

"Crap, Akbar. Do you have to look so damned happy?"

"Yeah," Akbar raised their joined hands again. "Always second place, Tim. Number Two man on *my* jump stick. Now third wheel left standing out in the rain," he bent forward to kiss Laura's fingers right on her wedding ring.

Tim felt the blow as if it had gone straight to his gut. If he'd had more in his gut than ice tea, he'd probably have been sick from the power of it.

He didn't see the signal that passed between them. It was too fast, too effortless, too…couple-based. Laura somehow warned Akbar he'd crossed the line without her making any big deal of it. The two of them had moved on to some other level that Tim was no longer a part of.

"Shit! Sorry, man," Akbar really did look sorry. "Didn't come out right, Tim. Not at all."

"No problem," Tim should be laughing it off, would have even six months ago. But he wasn't. It was just normal teasing between them. They'd each slung far worse crap at each other. After you'd been through as many close calls on a fire as the two of them had, with no one else to rely on but each other, what did a few jibbing words mean. Despite that, this time it stung.

He looked up at Snoopy, but the dog was busy with battles of his own.

"No problem," he repeated. He rose to his feet and looked at the empty chair by Vern. Like a good friend, the man had laid the babe groundwork for him; a leggy brunette was already casually eyeing Tim. It was tempting, but lately—even on the nights he'd chosen to play the game—he had more often ended up in his own bed rather than some willing lady's. For a moment he wondered when that trend had begun. Since back before Akbar met Laura…which mean what? He shrugged it off.

He peeled a couple dollars out of his wallet and dropped them beside his half-finished ice tea.

"You two have a great week. Laura, you've got the best man I've ever known, even when he's an idiot. You hang on tight."

He whacked Akbar on top of the head for old-time's sake and headed for the door.

Akbar caught up with him out in the gray rain halfway to his truck.

"Hey Tim. You okay man? Look, what I said back there—"

"We're fine, Akbar. Just my own garbage I guess. Think maybe I'll go home."

"Up to the base? I'll come up later and we'll make some plans. Go fishing or something."

Home. Tim looked up into the rain and let the drops patter down on his face. He hadn't had a "home" in years; he'd just been living in temporary quarters. Jumpbases in Colorado, California, and now Oregon. And the last few years MHA had been running off-season contracts down in Australia which had been a kick. Australian women were much more relaxed than their American counterparts.

But home?

He looked back down at his friend and punched him hard on the arm.

"Ow! What was that for?" Akbar's solid smokie-fit frame didn't waver in the slightest despite the power Tim had put behind the blow.

"That was for finding such an amazing woman that you ruin it for the rest of us."

His grin was electric as always, "Yep! Jackpot on that one. Sure you want to go home? Come back in and have something to eat."

Tim wasn't hungry. The thought of one of the Doghouse's monster mushroom and bacon burgers with a smokie barbeque sauce—a Smokejumper Deluxe, just didn't do it for him.

Then he thought about a moose burger with onion rings back home at French Pete's and wondered if Carl had changed the grease in the fryer since the last time Tim had been in Alaska. It had been years, so the chances were at least fair.

"Thanks, buddy, but no thanks," Tim looked down at his friend. "It's time I went home. I'll call you from Alaska."

"Alaska?" The look of shock on Akbar's face just made it all the sweeter.

CHAPTER 3

*M*acy could feel the onion rings roiling in her stomach. The date had been holding its own until halfway through the meal.

Then Brett had laid the bomb that she would never escape as long as she lived in Larch Creek—no! It would survive right past her death and go on into town legend.

"So, Macy, why the hell did you bloody Billy at the altar anyway?"

Like she was supposed to have a good answer to what was wrong with *her* not with Billy. The list was manifold and she wasn't about to share even if she knew where to begin, which she didn't.

"I mean you're one of the prettiest girls in town. What the hell happened?"

Most of the town had been in on the public scene a mere six months ago. Macy arriving at the church thinking she'd found true love, Billy's busted nose spilling red all over her white dress, and no wedding. That's the part everybody knew.

The part that she'd kept to herself was Billy standing with her at the altar and asking her in a soft whisper, during the middle of the ceremony she'd written on her own because he'd been *too busy* to help, how she felt about "three ways" because there was this hot Russian chick who'd come across the Bering Sea in a small boat and was currently in Fairbanks fishing for a green card and—

Thankfully Mrs. Harada had taught her well in the twice weekly Kung Fu classes at the Grange Hall; Macy hadn't just bloodied his nose on the altar, she'd broken it bad. She hoped that the Fairbanks "hot chick" didn't like men with crooked noses and two missing front teeth for that was how Billy had left town with a dirty rag pressed to his face and a blown cleaning deposit on his rented tux.

Macy staged a wedding-dress funeral; a bonfire event held in the deep tundra for a party of one. She'd flown her Bell LongRanger helicopter out past Monkey Hot Springs, gotten good and drunk, had a major cry, and burned the dress.

She had returned to Larch Creek red-eyed, hung over, and done with men.

Word was, Billy had wisely moved on from Fairbanks to Juneau, which was more Lower Forty-eight than it was Alaska. No one expected him ever to return.

So why was she sitting here with Brett?

He was a nice enough guy. Had always been decent to her, even when she was busy being a pain-in-the-ass teenage girl in high school. But that's where it had always ended.

"You know what, Brett?"

"Why do I get the feeling I should take back my question about Billy?"

"No, it's not that. You're okay," never burn a bridge in a small town, at least not unless it was really deserved. "But this is so not gonna happen between us. How about we just enjoy the meal together?"

Brett nodded carefully, looked disappointed for a moment. Then, thinking about it, smiled for the first time that evening.

The rest of the meal went much more smoothly.

TIM HAD FORGOTTEN what a total pain-in-the-legs it was to get home.

It was the sort of thing you did your best to block out, and he had succeeded. If he'd remembered, he might still be at the Doghouse.

He always had a kit bag behind the seat of the truck, so that had saved him driving back up to camp. An hour later he'd arrived at the Portland airport.

Smokejumper planes weren't really made for guys who were six-foot-four, but they figured you had a lot of gear. As long as he watched his head there weren't any real leg room problems.

The Alaska Airlines Dash-8 jet was made for people smaller than Akbar's five-six. Twelve-year-old kids wouldn't fit in these seats. He'd barely survived the forty minutes to Seattle. The leg up to Anchorage on a 787 had been at least tolerable, but scrunching himself up into another Dash-8 puddle jumper to Fairbanks for another hour-plus had him near suicidal. By the time he was faced with the broken seat adjuster on the last SUV on the rental lot, he'd downshifted to a stony resignation. They offered him a compact—no way his legs or his head would fit—or a mini-van. No way his pride would fit.

"That's what coming home does to you," he told his mangled legs as he drove out of the city and only took two wrong turns before finding the road out to Larch Creek; the new Goldhill subdivision threw him off and the small turn sign had gone missing as usual.

But as he climbed up over Liga Pass and Denali shone like a white fist punching into the sky out of the dark green that coated the mid-summer landscape, something shifted in him.

He rolled down the window and knew that smell. Not just the tall larch trees underlaid by a carpet of yellow daisy and bright fireweed, but also the bite on the air of the deep grasses going dry under the long summer days. The short Alaskan fire season was going to be brutal this year.

As a smokie, he followed weather reports the way couch potatoes followed sports scores. And Alaska was running for a hot-and-dry record this year. High eighties in the heartland didn't feel hot like the nineties in Oregon, instead it felt dangerous.

Once he'd crested Liga Pass, the heat eased off to seventies and the grasses were greener. Even from sixty miles away Denali and the Alaska Range were making their influence felt.

He twisted back down off the pass and rolled through Heinrich's barley fields and hoped that the old man had finally taken on an assistant. Carl brewed the best beer in the fifty states with Heinrich's barley, but the old German had to be eighty if he was a day. The crop looked like it was off to a good start this year at least.

Town was on him before he expected. Not that there were new houses, but rather that there were so few outliers. When Denali was doing the other half of her job, the mid-winter half, a soul didn't want to be too far out in the wind, except for folks like Clement who were all the way out in Tena.

He spotted Mom's truck out in front of French Pete's and pulled in. It was a bright blue Toyota pickup like almost everyone else's in town—the blue theme was something he'd never quite understood. But the bumper stickers were the giveaway. On one it said, *I kill people for a living*, with "Mystery Writer" in small print. On the other there was a large picture of a bright red fish and it stated, *This is a red herring.*

Tim had left Hood River before lunch, traveled for too damn many hours and an extra time zone, and his stomach insisted that he needed to eat something more than a tiny bag of over-salted almonds and he needed to do it now. For a change his connections had been too good to hit a food court anywhere along the way.

French Pete's looked exactly the same outside and in.

The Sunday gang was at the big corner table and he headed straight over. His mom actually screamed when she spotted him. She was a small woman, taking after her own Vietnamese mother rather than granddad who was still a big Oklahoma boy even in his eighties, jumped up on her chair and gave him a big hug. Most of his looks came from her, except every inch of his height and then some had come from granddad and his own French-Canadian father.

He held her close.

This was what it felt like to be home.

MACY'S DATE was dead and done.

She was just saying goodbye and thanking Brett for being decent about the whole thing; her fiancé—prior to the broken nose and missing teeth—had been a very popular man in Larch Creek. It was on the verge of becoming awkward when there was a shriek of delight that had both her and Brett stumbling out of their booth to look.

Over at the table where Dad had been sitting with his writing friends—and where she'd expected to finish off this evening—a towering figure was hugging Eva Harada. Even standing on her chair, the woman was shorter than he was. There was no question who it might be. Tim Harada had passed five feet by third grade and six feet before high school. He'd made the Larch Creek Snow Angels unbeatable in basketball four years running.

Tim and her big brother Stephen had been an unstoppable forward force, both on and off the court. The two of them had always swept the field whether the game was basketball, video, or dating.

Macy was not going to think about Tim. When Stephen had died in Afghanistan, Tim had made it home for the funeral, but stopped coming home after that. It had hurt. She'd lost her big brother twice, in some ways.

While she'd never thought of Tim as her big brother, not even a little, it was clear that was how he'd always seen his role in her life. He'd zealously guarded the outspoken girl who was always in trouble with someone about something. Tim had fished her out of even more scraps and scrape-ups than Stephen had. He was the one who had dragged her into his mom's Kung Fu class, "If you're going to be such a pain in the butt, you better learn how to survive it." The guy couldn't even swear decently, but he'd always been on her side.

It wasn't until he was gone that she'd missed him. Missed him like a hole had been chopped in her heart.

On his last couple visits, she'd been off at college in Juneau and then flight school in Anchorage. She would come home and find that everyone was talking about Tim-this and Tim-that. His smoke-jumping had taken on mythic proportions. Actually, Mount Hood Aviation's firefighting reputation had even reached up here and being on the lead stick meant that mythic might be about right.

It had been a long time since he'd been home and far longer since she'd seen him.

Well, she didn't need him back now.

She hooked her arm through Brett's elbow.

"If you want to walk me home, that would be nice. Just don't think it means anything, Brett."

"Sure, Mace."

She liked that he fell back to her old nickname. It was comfortable, an old childhood nickname that rarely surfaced any more. And, she realized with chagrin, it was one that Tim Harada had tagged her with after she'd chased him around the yard swinging a two-by-four. She'd been six and he ten, and he'd teased her so far past tolerance that he would have soundly deserved it if she had caught him.

"Like a rabid knight with a mace," he'd told Stephen that night over dinner. She'd at least had the satisfaction of planting a hard kick to his shin under the table.

She turned her attention back to Brett, "Didn't Linda Lee always have a soft spot for you? Seems to me she did. She just divorced that guy from Talkeetna and is coming back. I bet she could use a friendly shoulder when she comes in next week."

She half listened to Brett's surprised reply of "Really? She did?" as they stepped out through the door. Men just didn't have a clue.

The other half of her attention was noticing that Tim had sat right down at the table and was welcomed as if he'd never been away.

Tim had always fit in.

Well, she didn't need to be hurt by him. She knew his pattern from the stories. Hit town for a few days, and then bail. Men *so* didn't have a clue.

She gave Brett her full attention as they headed down the steps and strolled together under the long summer sunset that lasted past midnight this time of year.

THE PIECES DIDN'T CLICK in Tim's brain until after she was out the door; he'd barely seen her silhouette just for a second, but the way she moved was so familiar.

Mace Tyler.

He almost rose to chase after her. Give her a hug, maybe dunk her in the old claw-foot bathtub that served as a horse trough in front of the Zani's General Store. But his mom and her friends were so glad to have him among them that he stayed put. It was nice to know Mace was around, he'd missed her the last few times and was sorry for that.

It had always been a pinch that he hadn't been there more for her in the years since Stephen's death. Hell, he even remembered when she was born. Stephen became a big brother at the age of four and had very seriously asked Tim to help him so he didn't mess up. They'd made a spit-and-handshake swear on it, and here was Tim letting him down.

It was hard, being in this town and expecting to bump into his best friend around every corner. It must have been worse for her. Stephen would be pretty darn ticked at Tim right about now.

Well, he'd try to make it up to her this week.

So, staying beside his mom, who had her hand clamped in his, he tuned into the latest stories about the changing world of publishing. He was always surprised at how many famous authors had gathered in this little town. Mom and her bloody murder mysteries had been one of the first. Her in-residence Mastermind Meetings for pros at Stephanie's B&B had attracted others to make the change permanent.

Tim had always preferred reading Kim and Sam's action and adventure books to his mother's bloody mysteries, not realizing until he was much older that the books they were actually romances. The bare-chested men on the covers should have been a giveaway, but he'd liked all of the helicopter and airplane stuff from Kim's days flying Air Rescue with 920th Operations Group and Sam's with the Coast Guard. As a kid, he'd always just flipped past the "weird" stuff...until he'd hit puberty. After that he kind of switched which parts he paid attention to.

Macy's mom, Lisa, was still writing science fiction with her husband—under his name. They'd just pulled down their third Hugo and fourth movie.

"Got a question for you," Tim spoke up when there was a lull in the conversation after analyzing the clause changes in Mitch's latest thriller contract. "Does Larch Creek have the highest per capita rate of famous authors on the planet?"

"Famous? Don't know that any of us are famous other than your mom and the Tylers," Kim had always been the humble one of the couple.

Sam winked at him, "We keep a low profile. The wonders of pen names and a small community, everyone here knows not to reveal our secret identities to strays and out-of-towners."

Tim didn't point out that he and his wife were wearing matching t-shirts that proclaimed, *I'm a Romance Writer. What's Your Superpower?*

"There are eight of us here every Sunday dinner; that's over one in a hundred," Mitch observed.

"Don't forget Dorothy," his mom reminded them. "She may be getting on, and we don't see her as much, but she certainly still turns out that dark urban fantasy stuff—hot, sexy, and bloody. Gives me the shivers."

Everyone laughed that it was the murder mystery writer who was creeped out by Dorothy's tales. The woman was old enough to be Tim's grandmother, maybe great-grandmother.

"Maybe she's part vampire. Does she still come to the winter meetings?" Tim asked.

They all eyed each other and then burst out laughing. Dorothy's preference for nighttime was notorious. "Daylight hours is for writing," she'd always say.

"This," Mitch waved around his big hand and continued with a thick Texan accent, "is about as out and about as any of us want to be. That's the problem with counting authors, we're recluses by nature. Never was much a one for the social whirl of Austin. Always gave me the creeps a bit, meeting fans at signings and such," his shiver was much like Tim's mom's. "Might even be a couple around we don't know about. Carol said as how there was a package from a New York publisher she delivered to the new guy in the old Sharpton place."

Clement sat at the far end of the table and, as usual, didn't say much, but he nodded in agreement.

They were tight, Tim realized. They were as tight as the MHA smokie crew, but for different reasons. Rather than fire, adrenaline, and youth, this group shared a passion for stories. Some had arrived as Eva Harada's students for whom she'd stood as mentor at some workshop she'd taught on the "outside"—typically Fairbanks. Others had wandered through and come to a halt in Larch Creek or Tena much to their own surprise.

"Come for a week and stay for a lifetime," Tim commented drily and earned a good laugh.

"That mean you're home for good this time, Timmy boy?"

"No way, Mitch," Tim held up both hands to fend off the idea as Carl brought him a fresh pint of barley beer, a venison steak, and a stack of honey-gold onion rings. "It's rainy this week in the Lower Forty-eight. They gave us some days off for bad behavior and I decided I hadn't seen Mom's face in too long."

He let the pause hang while he sipped his beer.

His audience, a crowd of storytellers, knew when a story was only half finished.

"Of course if I'd known the first familiar face I'd see in town would be yours, Mitch…"

The laughter was good. Made him forgive the airlines for folding him up like a pretzel to get here. At least a little bit.

CHAPTER 4

oming off the fire, Tim should be out of it for another dozen-hour night of sleep, but the Alaskan summer light did things to you. Running on three to four hours sleep just seemed natural this time of year and even a half decade away hadn't changed that old pattern. Of course if he'd remembered to close the blackout curtains in his childhood bedroom it might have helped.

Three-thirty in the morning and he was wide awake. His old room faced to the east, so the sun punched directly into his face making him squint as he struggled to find fresh clothes in his kit bag. It was a good thing he'd left a jacket here, he'd forgotten that Larch Creek in the summer wasn't all that much warmer than Oregon in the winter.

When he tried to pull it on, the old denim barely fit.

Last time he'd worn it was his rookie summer as a hotshot eight years ago. Despite having a long, lean frame, like every other person who worked wildfire he'd bulked up over the season. And the last two years with MHA he'd fought the Australian season as well. His good polar fleece was still down at the MHA camp in Oregon.

He struggled with his favorite jacket a moment longer then hung it back on the door and opted for a sweater he'd left in the old dresser because it was too warm for the Lower Forty-eight. It was too heavy, but Ms. Maypole had knit it just for him so the sleeves were right on his long arms without the body having the bulk of a triple-XL. It would do until he could hit a store in Fairbanks.

His room was unchanged. A pile of plastic trophies for basketball and track-and-field. Posters that proved his teenage taste in music had nothing to do with the music and everything to do with how hot the solo female vocalist was. Most of them weren't even on his playlist anymore.

It had started with Madonna, despite her being older than his mother—a comparison he wasn't liking at the moment. Even though he still listened to her sometimes, he pulled the thumbtacks and rolled her up. Then Britney followed her. Gaga, Aguilera, Swift when she was about fourteen. Whitney and Mariah came down as well. Tina Turner was a classic, but older than his grandmother; what had he been thinking? Soon they were all down and his walls looked strangely barren.

All that was left was the "picture window" as he'd always called it— a big corkboard his dad had helped him mount years ago. It was covered with photos. Mostly his family...and Stephen Tyler. It was rare to have a photo of him without Stephen.

And even rarer to have a photo of the two of them without Mace Tyler stuck in the background somewhere. The picnic up on Sushana River where they'd all nearly died of blood loss to the mosquitoes, at least it had felt that way and the three of them had certainly looked it—bright red with bites despite gallons of bug spray. There she was, front seat on the school bleachers during a basketball game when the Snow Angels had trounced the Fairbanks Nanooks. He and Stephen dressed for the prom, and the gawky eighth-grader Mace sandwiched between them for the pre-event photo.

He'd figure out what to put up on the rest of the walls later, if anything.

Tim tapped Mace's nose in the prom photo, because it used to drive her stone cold nuts when he did it in real life. He wondered if it

32

still did? He should try it and find out. Actually, her vengeance had always been lethal, so maybe not.

The upstairs of the house was quiet as he snuck down. Q2 the cat —who he'd named for the Star Trek character, Q the First was buried out under a blueberry bush—was curled up in a corner of the living room so close to the wood stove that it was always a surprise he didn't spontaneously combust.

"Getting lazy there, boy," Tim gave him a scritch that Q2 barely bothered to wake up for. Even as a kitten the little beast had known better than to let something as trivial as attention interfere with a good nap. Lazy was the cat's middle name, only the sound of kibble striking his cat bowl broke through that nonplussed attitude.

Dad was still out cold or there would be coffee on the stove. He could hear Mom already typing away in her office. It could be hours, or even days before she surfaced, depending on where she was in the next book; and interrupting her when she was on a roll ranked as an unacceptable safety risk.

Tim eased out into the morning sunshine of central Alaska. Again, the air was so different here. Even though the MHA camp was high on the face of Mount Hood and claimed some of the freshest air in the state as it rolled down off the high glaciers, Central Alaska was different. It was so fresh that it felt as if it had been just created.

Not quite sure why, Tim crunched himself into the SUV and drove down into Larch Creek rather than walking. Carl opened French Pete's when he woke up. If you got there before he was up and about, he didn't mind someone else going in and starting the coffee.

Four in the morning, the sun already a handspan above the valley walls, the town was awake. No one was doing any of the noisy work; that was just plain rude before six, but folks were out and about. They'd squint at his strange car, stark in its rental whiteness, and then wave cheerily when they spotted his face practically mashed up against the windshield. He needed to go by Mark's and see if the mechanic could fix the seat for him, but the garage would still be locked up.

Despite his need for coffee Tim drove past French Pete's, "Just seeing the old town again" he told himself. He was most of the way to the Tyler's house, just to sort of see if Mace was awake yet or—

Stephen's truck was parked at the old Mason place. It was the same blue as most other trucks in town, but he remembered the night they'd put that big dent in the side panel.

It jolted him to a stop with a loud skid on the coarse gravel.

He could only stare at it.

Not possible—

Then he spotted the bumper sticker which declared: *My Other Car Is A Bell LongRanger!* And the other: *Auntie Em, There's No Craft Like Rotorcraft!*

Mace must have taken Stephen's truck after he died.

The cottage, which had been a run down piece of crap that Mason had never kept up for one moment in the forty years he'd been there, was so transformed he barely recognized it. Now it was a neat little cottage with a copper-toned metal roof and a garden busy with flowers.

Sitting out on the front porch, eyeing him like he was a total lunatic, was Mace Tyler and a knee-high-sized dog that looked part lab and part husky.

Tim left the SUV where it was, Buck Street didn't have anything fancy like a curb to pull up to. He clambered out and waved.

Mace didn't wave back.

Crap! Tim hadn't expected her to be that mad at him.

MACY TRIED TO WAVE BACK, she really did. But one hand held her mug and the other was convulsively clenched deep in Baxter's fur.

Tim stuffed his hands in his pockets and moseyed up the walkway.

Baxter let out a low growl. It was just his "I don't know you" noise, but it was enough to stop Tim a half dozen paces away. The man was absolutely not supposed to look so good, and so familiar. He'd been her first memory, sitting on the floor beside her, teaching her how to stack building blocks. She'd had a crush on him since...she was born —for all the good it had done her. Well, she could at least be civilized.

"Hey, Tim."

"Hey yourself. That still hot chocolate or do you drink grown up drinks now?"

She looked down at the mug and felt like she was twelve, "Hot chocolate."

"With or without?" he grinned down at her.

"With, of course," and she tried not to feel like she was six. "Who in their right mind would drink hot chocolate without the little marshmallows?" Other than Tim Harada. She tried to make it sound fierce but the sentence didn't really lend itself to that very well.

He moved up to the start of the porch steps and squatted down until he was almost eye to eye with Baxter then held out his knuckles.

"Watch it, he's fierce."

Baxter sniffed his hand and then licked it.

"Yep," Tim agreed far too casually. "As fierce as Old Jake," the prior family mutt who had also turned into a total mush whenever Tim came around.

Baxter had so hated Billy that she'd come close to finding him a new home before the wedding. That hadn't happened. Big clue there.

Oh, please don't let Tim have heard about that.

"Looks nice," Tim nodded to the house. "You do the work yourself?"

"Yes. Why?" she hadn't meant to snap at him, but this sentence picked up the heat she'd been missing earlier.

"Looks well done, Mace. That's why. When did you acquire the patience to do decent trim work and painting?"

"You've been gone a while, Tim."

And his face shifted as if she'd just hauled off and punched him in the gut. It lost color and the easy full-of-himself smile was gone as if it had never been.

"What?"

Tim was staying focused on scratching Baxter's head. The dog was stretching out his neck for more of it, the traitor. He dragged her hand, which was still anchored in the dog's ruff, right under Tim's.

He didn't jerk back like she wanted to.

Instead he rested his hand over hers deep in Baxter's fur and looked up at her with those forest dark eyes of his.

"I'm sorry I haven't been..." he stalled, looked up at the sky as if hunting for what he'd meant to say, "...around more. You know. Since...Stephen." Then he squeezed her hand a final time and withdrew it.

Baxter whined when Tim rose back to his feet. The couple steps up the porch were not enough to make up for Tim's height and he was once again looking down at her.

"If you...need anything. Just let me know."

He scuffed a boot on her gravel walkway.

"Well, I should be going," he nodded to her, brushed his fingertips over Baxter's nose, and turned to head back to his truck.

She gaped at him. Men weren't clueless; they were incomprehensible.

He was trying to fold himself back into his rental when she finally shook off the paralysis. She jerked to her feet, splashing hot cocoa on her hand which made her curse, and released her hold on Baxter.

He jumped off the steps and bounded down to Tim. When Tim turned to pet him again, Baxter moved right in to sniff, jamming that big snout of his right up between Tim's legs. Baxter was barely tall enough, but he connected.

With a *whoosh* and a pinching together of his legs, Tim stumbled back against the SUV and clipped the back of his head on the door frame.

Baxter thought that was very entertaining and jumped up to place two husky-sized paws on Tim's thighs, pinning him half in—half out of the vehicle.

Macy set her hot cocoa down on the porch, wiped her hand on her jeans, and moved up behind Baxter, but made no effort to call him off. She wanted to lay into Timothy Harada. Shout what an idiot he was. Tell him...things she'd never told anyone. She needed a different tack.

"You know, these seats are adjustable," it was in the full forward position and even she wouldn't be able to fit her five-ten frame into the tiny space.

Tim was making a poor attempt to rub the back of his head with one hand and fend off Baxter trying to crawl up and lick his face with the other.

It was odd, Baxter didn't generally like strangers.

"Not this one," he managed to shove Baxter down. If Tim had thought to say "Sit," Baxter would have obeyed immediately. But like most of the writers, the Haradas were cat people. "It's broken, but this was the last decent car on the rental lot."

She snapped her fingers and Baxter immediately dropped to his butt. She shoved Tim aside and looked under the seat. She worked the release lever a few times and spotted the problem. She pulled her multi-tool out of her back pocket.

THIS WAS NOT the Mace Tyler that Tim had always known. Sure, she was still far too sure that she was right—which she usually was. There'd never been any question where the brains of the family had landed. Of both their families.

But she lived in a picture postcard house, which didn't sound like her at all, and was presently leaning down into his truck with her butt facing him. Her jeans were worn almost to holes and were so soft that they traced every curve. The outline of where the multi-tool lived was a white imprint on the worn denim. Her position emphasized things that Stephen would beat the crap out of him for noticing if he were still around.

Mace the girl from childhood had been replaced by Macy Tyler the stunning woman. Mace, no—Macy had changed. Not that he'd ever say her proper name out loud or she'd know for sure something strange was going on between his "tall ears" where, she never failed to remark "he occasionally resorted to vain attempts at creating a cognitive process."

Tim tried to look somewhere else, but ended up facing the dog who was clearly wondering what his problem was. When he turned, Baxter went for the nose ram again and Tim was barely fast enough to get a blocking hand up. Knowing Macy, she'd probably trained the dog to do just that.

With an abrupt ratcheting sound, the seat slid back and thunked against the last stop. There was the sharp clunk as it locked into place.

"Oh my god! You're a savior, Tyler."

She stood up with that smarmy grin on her face.

He wrapped her in a quick hug.

She went stiff as a spruce tree.

He backed off and mumbled a soft, "Sorry."

Her face was unreadable in the moment before she brushed him aside to escape from where he'd inadvertently trapped her between the SUV and the open door.

"I owe you, Mace."

"You don't owe me squat," she sounded pissed as a balked wildfire as she tromped back to the porch and picked up her hot cocoa. She stood with her back to him. Not that he was enjoying the view or anything.

"Okay, fine," he needed something light to defuse whatever was going on. "My legs owe you though. They were on the verge of staging a rebellion and quitting the service after three plane flights and then that front seat."

"Great! If I ever need your legs, I'll give them a call. Now go back wherever you came from."

Tim leaned back against the truck, kept half an eye on Baxter, and the other one-and-a-half on Macy Tyler.

She snapped her fingers and Baxter raced to her side. She gathered up her hot chocolate mug and they went inside with a slam of the screen door.

Tim knew what he would do...if it was anyone other than Macy. Go up and knock. Say something sweet and smooth and funny like, "I have another problem that needs fixing. There's this kid sister of my best friend who hates me for reasons unknown..." Well, not the best ploy, but he could always come up with something; he did best when it was on the fly.

Except this was Macy.

He'd obviously hurt her and hurt her badly by not being around since Stephen enlisted and didn't come back.

Storming the fortress wasn't going to work.

He climbed back into the rental and headed down to French Pete's for breakfast. It would take some thinking, but he had to find a way to make it up to her.

MACY DID her best not to scream as she listened to Tim drive off. And she hadn't watched from the window because she sure wasn't going to give him the satisfaction. Plus, it was too lame for words.

She shoved her mug in the microwave, but didn't bother turning it on. Instead she crossed her arms to glare at it. For one thing, the marshmallows would get all weird. And the handle too hot. Microwaves never reheated hot chocolate properly.

Couldn't she do anything right?

"I know how to hug a man, don't I?"

Baxter sat on the floor and looked longingly from her to the dog biscuit drawer and then back to her.

"I hugged Brett normal as could be just last night, didn't I? He didn't even try to cop a feel."

Was it because he was decent or Macy was a psycho woman with…

"No! Not finishing that sentence."

Baxter gave up and sighed as he lay on the wood of the old floor.

But how was she supposed to hug Tim Harada normally?

On one hand, he was family. She'd been in his arms a thousand times, everything from tackle football to practicing for a school dance to shoving him when he least expected if a large mud puddle presented itself as too tempting a target. He was quick and half the time she'd go in with him, but it was always worth it; sometimes it was even better that way.

So why had she gotten all weird this time?

She pulled down cereal for her breakfast, but could smell that the milk had turned the moment she uncapped the bottle. Pancakes...required milk. Eggs...she was out of. Oatmeal with soymilk wasn't quite as awful as it sounded, but it was close. She'd shed her Pop Tart addiction two years ago and there wasn't a one in the cupboards.

"Fine! Breakfast out, Baxter."

He knew those words and raced to the door to wait. Carl always had a bowl of meat scraps in the fridge.

Normally they'd walk, but she had a mail flight in another hour, so she took the truck. She rolled down the driver's window despite the chill morning air and drove off, calling for Baxter to run close behind and get a couple of the kinks out with a six-block run as she drove over.

She was climbing out of the truck, when she heard a shout of, "Heads up!"

Macy turned barely in time to see Baxter leap in front of her and grab a Frisbee just moments before it whacked her in the nose.

The dog bounded up the steps and dropped it at Tim's feet. He was part way down the cluttered porch, but Baxter reached him and then bounded back into view, ready to race after the next throw.

Tim leaned out, off balance over the porch rail, and heaved the disk with an underhand throw that sent it soaring down the middle of the Parisian Way, skipping off the top of Herb Maxwell's truck and floating most of the way to the hardware store.

Baxter snagged it inches from the ground at the cost of doing a full somersault. But he came up with it in his teeth and was already trotting it back to Tim.

She flashed a signal and Baxter turned at the last moment and delivered it to her. With a sharp overhand she sent it whipping at Tim's face. Hard.

He trapped it with a solid *thunk* against his palms, grinned, and winged it further the other way up the street toward the church.

Baxter raced, leapt for the catch, and returned. He stopped halfway between them and eyed them both with the Frisbee still clamped in his teeth.

Tim waved for Baxter to give it to Macy, and he obeyed. He'd never obeyed anyone but her.

"It's Stephen's," he called down from the porch. "Or maybe it was mine, but it's the one we kept underneath the butter churn in case we were in town and wanted to play."

Macy took it and could feel almost feel her brother's hands on it. Frisbee was the big summer sport in Larch Creek. Arable land was too precious in the valley to waste any of it on a football or soccer field. There was the softball field, with the outside wall of the school's gym filling in as a vertical outfield. Above the faded white line painted at ten feet high was a triple, above the line at twenty feet up the wall was a home run.

Frisbee, they could play it anywhere. It bounced off windows without damage and if it went into the river, there was always a dog willing to swim for it. Snowshoe Ultimate had been a serious winter workout game.

But this one had been Stephen's. Stephen and Tim's.

Most of the anger drained out of her. She flicked it lightly up to Tim who momentarily disappeared from view as he tucked it back under the butter churn.

"How about breakfast?" he asked when he reappeared. "My treat."

"Firefighting must pay well."

"Well enough," he aimed that lethal smile down at her and then began working his way across the porch as she climbed the steps. They reached the front door at the same time.

Tim held the door for her like she was a lady, something Brett had missed at every opportunity. She scoffed at Tim which seemed the appropriate response.

———

TIM SMILED and waited for Macy to enter first. Her eye roll was so familiar that he almost reached out to "beep" her nose, but she was gone inside before he had the chance.

At five a.m. in mid-July, French Pete's was about a quarter full. There was no factory or anything in town, it was simply summer near the Arctic Circle and a lot of folks were up. They sat in groups of two and three and were mostly quiet over coffee. Carl had never been a big believer in music and the local radio station wouldn't be on the air for a couple of hours, assuming Janice was still running it.

Tim breathed in deep. The air was thick with deer sausage, warm syrup, and toad-in-a-hole—a single egg fried in a hole torn in the middle of a slice of toast. Carl made it with the good dark bread. Herb Maxwell came in after closing and worked through the night to bake it when Carl didn't need the ovens for anything else. It was a whole world of good that Tim had forgotten even existed.

Tim headed for their old booth, dropped into it, and only then realized what he'd done.

"Damn! Sorry, Mace. You pick where," he started to get up, but she dropped in across from him.

"This is fine."

Tim struggled back into place and tried not to feel too weird about knocking knees with Macy. He shifted to the inside on his side to get some clear foot space; which was Stephen's usual spot. Tim typically sat to the outside so that he could stretch out his legs, but the dog was already curled up there.

Macy was watching him fidget with that strangely blank expression, making it so that he barely recognized her.

"Stop it," she told him softly.

"Stop what?" Tim froze.

"He's been dead for five years, just stop being so twitchy."

Tim tried. He put his hands flat on the table and simply stopped. Akbar was always the one busy about something and Tim the quiet and steady one of the pair, or at least by comparison. He and Stephen had been the same way.

"Sorry. I'm—"

"An idiot," Macy finished for him. "But we know that about you already. He's been dead a long time and I've had to let him go. Stop jumping at every goddamn ghost."

"Sorry," he held up a hand as she opened her mouth. "I know. Apologizing too much. I just—" Tim looked at the ceiling where his old model airplane with the tiny gas engine presently hung upside down, which was the poor thing's usual position in flight—Tim had been an expert at crashing. He'd wondered what happened to the thing after he'd stopped fooling around with it in favor of girls.

He looked across at Macy. Sometimes the straight line was the best one at bars, maybe he should try it here when it mattered.

"I really am sorry I haven't been around. I feel like I've let down both you and Stephen by not being here for you more often."

"Are you really that dumb?"

He looked down at Baxter who was also wondering the same thing, but Tim suspected him of food-based bias. It still didn't give him a clue why he was being dumb. He turned back to Macy.

"Apparently, yes."

She rolled her eyes in that way of hers that always made him feel particularly stupid. "I'm a big girl, Harada. Don't need six feet plus of gawk to protect me from anything."

"Maybe not. But I still think of you as the kid sister and my natural, in-born notion of decency says that if you need anything, I want to be the one that's there for you. I feel like crap for how I've treated you since Stephen died."

Macy closed her eyes and thudded her forehead on the table as Carl came up with two mugs of hot chocolate, one with marshmallows, one without. Tim had long since switched over to coffee in the mornings, but didn't see any point in making a fuss.

"Problem?" Carl asked Tim as Macy continued thunking her head.

"No. Seems about normal. I'll take two toad-in-a-holes with a side of bacon and another of the deer sausage."

Macy looked up at him.

"What? I'm a growing boy doing a man's job. Firefighting is hungry work."

Macy sighed, "Give me what he's having, but half as much."

Carl patted Macy's shoulder as if telling her to be strong before he moved off.

Tim wondered what that was about.

Macy checked in with herself. Weak spot in her brain for Tim Harada still installed? Yep! There for everyone to see plain as day except for Tim? Check. Even Carl, the least sympathetic guy on the planet, could see it and was trying to console her?

Shit!

She looked Tim square in the eye, "I'm. Not. Your. Kid. Sister."

"Says you," he offered one of those casual grins that he always thought were so charming. That it was, didn't help matters in the slightest.

He still saw her that way? She had no hope at all.

"You're stuck with me, Mace. Not a thing you can do about it."

"At least for this week," *and then you'll be gone again.*

He had the decency to shift uncomfortably.

"My job is in the Lower Forty-eight."

Hard to argue. And her life was here. She rubbed her forehead and sipped some cocoa. Tim was trying to be civil and she was the one being a total bitch.

Another thing that was never going to change. Well, maybe she'd try.

"Tell me about it."

"My job?"

"Sure. Why do you jump fire? Adrenalin rush? Bragging rights? All of the hot women?" Why she'd said the last, she'd never know. So that she could flog herself with the image of Tim in another woman's arms?

"There's that," his happy smile almost had her leaving the table.

Probably would have if Carl hadn't returned at that moment with her plate, Tim's platter, and a bowl for Baxter. She could leave her own meal, but she wouldn't do that to her dog.

"But the real reason is probably Akbar the Great."

"Who?"

"My jump partner. He and I started as hotshots together. He got this hair up his behind to go for jump school. 'Big bucks and hot women,' he'd say. I ended up following him in."

"He actually calls himself 'the Great'?"

Tim nodded, "Everyone does. His first name actually means 'the Great' in some language or other. So really he's actually 'The Great the Great.' He earns it though, he's the best smokejumper you can imagine. Fires run and hide when Akbar is jumping them. Can't be more than five-six, but with a pro-wrestler's shoulders and a smile that really lights the ladies up."

"So you and he really cut a swath," she kept her attention down on her breakfast. She had no idea how she could eat, her stomach hurt worse than it had during last night's date with Brett.

"Used to, yeah," he hacked into his first toad-in-a-hole.

"What happened?" her curiosity had her looking up; all the way up. There was a surprising mix of sadness and confusion on his features. She'd always been able to read Tim and these were real emotions, deep ones; the kind he didn't let out very often.

"He found a lady."

"Why is that a bad thing?"

"What? No. Laura is amazing. Smart, beautiful, funny. She's way too good for him."

"So? What happened?" she took a sip of her hot chocolate.

"He married her."

She practically snorted the scalding liquid out her nose. Set herself to hacking and coughing until he solicitously handed her some water.

Once she recovered, she managed to ask, "And...?"

"Huh?"

Tim really didn't get it, "The look on your face."

"What look? Laura's the best damn thing that could happen to the twerp."

"But..." It was like pulling teeth. Macy went for some bacon. That seemed to go down okay.

Tim scratched at his chin. He hadn't shaved that morning and it added to his slightly lost look.

She could feel her brain going soft on him and even though she knew it was a path to a world of hurt, she couldn't stop it.

"I don't know. He and I, when we had a break, we'd go down to the Doghouse," he looked around, "which is only a little more respectable than this place, and we'd—" He finally caught himself and realized what he was saying. He blushed. Tim actually blushed as if she was still twelve and he'd said things he shouldn't in front of a little girl.

"You don't get off that easy, Harada. Give."

He did that intimidating glare thing that he'd never understood only served to peak her curiosity.

"Give."

"Fine!" he slapped down his knife and fork hard enough to earn a startled look from Baxter. "Yesterday, was it just yesterday? Yeah, maybe. We came off a hellacious fire. Ten days, eighty thousand acres, a hundred kinds of ugly."

"But you beat it?"

"But we beat it. And when I cruise into the Doghouse, there's the usual gang doing the usual thing with all the cute women in the bar."

Macy did her best *not* to imagine it, but didn't succeed very well.

"And over to one side there are Akbar and Laura being all…" he flapped his hands like when he was really perplexed.

"What?"

"Happy together!"

"Still not getting why that's a bad, Harada." She was really having a problem following this, but then, apparently, so was Tim.

"No. It's good. Great! I'm really, honestly happy for him. They're an amazing couple. Hell, I stood as best man for him."

An actual expletive from Timothy Harada, he must really be flummoxed. "And you took home a bridesmaid or two?"

"That's not the point." His look said he had, but he didn't elaborate and she didn't want to know.

"Then what is?"

Tim dragged his hands through his hair and then looked at her. Really looked at her as if seeing her for the first time.

"I wish I knew, Mace. I turned around and there's this brunette eyeing me—the kind with legs that never stop, and I just walked out. Next thing I know I'm sitting here with you and I haven't a clue why."

Macy couldn't help herself. She reached out and brushed a hand over his cheek.

The sweet boy was still there, sitting across from her. Lost, tucked away, hidden by the man he'd become, but he was still there. And it broke her heart, for that was the Tim she'd always been in love with.

Against all odds he still existed, and in a week he'd be gone again.

CHAPTER 5

im felt strangely quiet through the rest of the meal, as if the chaos of his emotions had been burned away by Macy's touch.

The problem was that he now stood in the "black." It was the area that a forest fire had already been through, stripped of color by heat and flame until there was only the black of char, the gray of ash, and the blue of sky shining between leafless black branches. Flare-ups of spot fires might occur, and there were often surreal patches of green that the fire had swept all around but not burned. It was a quiet, almost serene space.

It was also a place where you stood after a fire, wrung out and half wondering what you were supposed to do next. Smokejumpers stayed ahead of the fire to cut it off. They only crossed into the black when they had to escape, or when the job was done.

Tim oddly felt as if he'd only just managed to escape, but he didn't know from what.

When Macy announced that she had a flight to make, he'd asked if he could ride along. It would be a good chance to see the surrounding area.

She'd looked surprised, even wary, but finally said he could come.

"No jumping out of my helicopter though. I don't carry parachutes."

Baxter had looked chagrined when he'd been relegated to the truck bed for the trip down to the hangars. They were tucked among the trees close beside the one straight stretch of the main road north of town. Power lines had been rerouted upslope and the shoulders to either side were all Heinrich's barley, so no trees stuck up to clip wings or rotor blades.

He helped Macy roll the Bell 206 LongRanger out of the hangar and onto the small paved space between the hangars and the road. MHA only flew the converted Black Hawks and the tiny MD500s. The LongRanger fell halfway between the two in size.

"Pretty," Tim couldn't help but whistle. The 206 was a long and sleek helicopter. A single, two-bladed rotor. The cockpit up front offered a great side-by-side view for pilot and copilot. Room for five in the back in facing seats. Luggage compartment. Cargo hook. It was easy to see why this craft was the first choice of news and police agencies.

"She's my baby. Mom and Dad gave me the loan to buy her and I expect to have it paid off before the end of the century," Macy patted the helo's nose and dropped the tow cradle down so that she was resting on her skids. "Glass avionics, high-altitude rotor, the whole bit."

"How high?" Tim hesitated.

Macy simply pointed at the mountain looming beyond the south end of the valley. It looked as if she was pointing at the top.

"You don't!" Part of his Type I Incident training had included a week-long mountain rescue course that had put the fear of god in him. That was fine when you had to rappel down a cliff face or fetch someone off the side of Mount Hood. But Denali was a whole different matter. He was the monster, the tallest peak in North America. The death toll on his flanks was three to five a year, except when he was in a bad mood which was most years.

Macy stood up from where she'd been inspecting the underside of the tail rotor as part of her pre-flight.

"I don't what?"

"You don't take tourists up—" He couldn't even choke out the words as he pictured her dead on the ice fields of Denali wrapped up in a snarl of sheet metal that had once been a helicopter.

She walked right up to him, fisted her hands on her hips, and stared up at him, "What if I do?"

"Are you an idiot?" It exploded out of him. Tim never lost his temper, but imagining Macy doing something stupid— "Do you know how many people die trying to fly up—" Then he saw that smile of hers. She'd never been able to quite lock it down when teasing him, which had saved him from looking the fool not a single time in their entire history together. He still fell for it. "Crap!"

She burst out laughing, finally laying a hand on his shoulder and shaking him a bit.

"Oh," she gasped out. "You should see your face."

"Double crap!"

"You never could swear worth a damn, Harada."

"Triple crap!" he grinned down at her.

"Shee-it!" she said in a way that would have made Akbar proud. "Tourists pay plenty for the scenic tour, but even I'm not crazy enough to fly them to the top. I have the high altitude rig for when mountain rescue places a call-out. I only go that high to save lives, not for dumb-ass joy rides."

"Still…" Tim could feel the nerves creep back up his spine.

Macy cursed, grabbed his arm, and dragged him around to the right hand pilot's door. She swung it open and fished out something from an inside pocket on the door and shoved it into his hands.

He opened the thin leather book as she returned to inspecting the helo. It was a logbook, but on the first page were her certifications from the Mountain Rescue Association—she had a lot of them, her Denali Park Service on-call information, and the contact numbers for the National Incident Management System—the same one that called out MHA on fires. She was even drop-certified on forest fires.

Tim flipped through the pages of the log as she continued her way around the helicopter. Mail run, mail run, tourist flight, tourist flight, rescue at Denali camp at seventeen thousand feet (wind forty knots / temp minus thirty), mail run, mail run, hunting party to Lake…

Again, when she came back around the nose of the aircraft, it was as if he was seeing her for the first time. She kept changing on him so fast he was having trouble keeping up. Last night she'd been the little girl he'd missed. This morning a grown-up he could make no sense of. And now…

For a moment, he saw the tall, slim woman with light skin and dark hair that floated off her shoulders. She wore dark sunglasses, but he knew her honey-brown eyes would be watching him even now because Macy never missed anything.

He wasn't comfortable seeing Macy Tyler as a beautiful woman, but now that he had, it was hard to stop. A flash of dragging her off into Heinrich's barley field left him supremely uncomfortable.

She finished her inspection and once more stood in front of him. She pulled the logbook from his nerveless fingers and tucked it back into the door pocket. He noticed that right next to it was a fire shelter in its pouch. All helicopter pilots who flew to wildfire kept one there in case they were downed too close to a blaze.

The thought of Macy Tyler in a deployed fire shelter was enough to give him nightmares.

"Crap, Mace. How did I get so far behind?"

"Been away a while, Flame Boy."

"Flame Boy?"

"C'mon, Harada. Johnny Storm, the Human Torch, Fantastic Four? Don't tell me you've forgotten all your comic books while you were away. Are you a total dweeb now?" Her greatest insult.

"Flame Boy?" he knew he sounded dense, but Macy as a woman still had his brain stupefied beyond functioning.

He barely saw her launch the punch in time to clench his gut. Still, much of the air whooshed out of his lungs for a moment. He'd forgotten how strong she was.

"Wow! Major gut muscles there, Mr. Storm. Bet you work out for a living."

He blinked down at her and tried to find a response. He really did.

"Now's your chance."

His chance for what?

She waited a moment before shaking her head and climbing aboard. Just before she shut the door she said, "Your door is on the other side, oh Dense One."

He opened his mouth and then shut it again and moved around to the passenger door on the left side of the cockpit. *His chance?* To what? Stop gaping like a beached salmon?

Baxter was sitting by the copilot's door waiting for him. He cracked it to ask Macy if the dog was coming or staying, and was almost butted aside onto the pavement, which answered that question.

Tim opened the rear side door to the five seats of the passenger cabin behind the cockpit.

Baxter gave him a second look as if to make sure that wasn't Tim's spot. The dog was also clearly used to riding next to his mistress. Tim gave him a nudge and he clambered aboard.

Tim shut the door on his "I'm a sad puppy" face and climbed in the left-side copilot's door.

There was a high-whine as Macy hit the starter that sliced right into his skull. He slammed the door which cut the noise by two-thirds.

"Wow! That was harsh."

Macy didn't respond. That's when he noticed she was wearing a double-earmuff headset with a boom mic. He scrabbled around looking for one.

"Under the seat," Macy yelled at him over the climbing noise. "Baxter doesn't wear them much. Chewed on them a bit as a puppy, but he's over that now. The noise doesn't seem to bother him."

He dug them out and clamped them on before the turboshaft engine rode up too loud. He also found a pair of sunglasses that weren't too scuffed up and pulled those on as well.

Once the rotor was pounding away, Macy switched on the headsets and he could hear her.

"You fly?"

"Only a little. Returning from a fire, if we got a lift from helitack, I try to get front seat. Nothing official."

"Let's see you do your stuff."

He looked at her as if she had lost her mind and almost got trapped in that dazzling smile.

Macy Tyler, very female, deftly handling heavy machinery, and with a smile brighter than the heart of a wildfire.

Yeah, now at least he knew what chance he'd passed up a moment ago…his last chance to turn and run.

MACY HAD to admit that she was enjoying screwing with Tim's head. He'd never had a single bone of sneaky in his body. Maybe that's how he swept up the bar babes so easily, by being so forthright about wanting them.

He wrapped those big hands of his around her helicopter's controls and she did her best to repress the warm shiver that slid up from where her hands rested on the matching set in front of her.

Oddly, it was his hands that had been the biggest change about him. That and the sadness. Both of those were new. He'd always been lean and athletic. Even now, bulked up with the work of smoke-jumping he was still lean, just powerful. But his hands, which had always been his most delicate feature, were now well callused and solid with muscle. As solid as his gut.

He tentatively moved the cyclic right and left, forward and back. She let her right hand ride along on the matching joystick that curved up to be positioned over her lap.

"Lighter feel than a Black Hawk."

"I've never flown one," and found herself a little ticked that he had. Black Hawks were masterful Type I machines that could heave a thousand gallons per load, over four tons of water or retardant. Her Bell 206 LongRanger, despite the L-4 modification of a larger engine, was classed as a Type III, and could heft only a few hundred gallons.

"Emily's Firehawk feels like a tank by comparison. I flew the

MD500 with Jeannie a couple times before she graduated to the Fire-hawk. That's a delicate craft."

Jeannie or the MD500? Macy did her best to ignore the stab of jealousy. Was it at his flying the Firehawk or had he also flown Emily and Jeannie as a part of the "training"?

"I always felt as if I was going to break her little helicopter. This just feels right, a nice place between the two others."

She wasn't going to ask. She wasn't. She wasn't!

Tim checked all around, and eased up on the collective with his left hand.

Macy could place his skill level instantly. None of the beginner flail, but no practiced smoothness either. He could fly basic patterns under perfect conditions and that would be about all. Still, he had no obvious bad habits—other than collecting women like bright pennies.

Tim climbed steadily and when she pointed a finger north, he managed a reasonable turn in that direction, though his rudder work needed some definite practice.

"So, does my baby fly as smooth as Emily or Jeannie?" Oh shit! She hadn't been going to say that. She really hadn't. Crap like that always just came out.

Tim burst out laughing.

Not quite the response she'd expected.

"Oh god. You'd have to meet them to know just how ludicrous that question is."

"Ugly hags?" she only wished.

"No, both stunning."

That would teach her. He continued apparently unaware of the level of shit he'd just left her to stew in. She wouldn't be jealous. There was nothing to be jealous of. Tim lived in the Lower Forty-eight. Women down there were all—

"Emily Beale is about the most terrifying woman you'd ever meet. She's a former Army Major."

"Couldn't cut it, huh?"

"Former Night Stalker."

Well, that finally put the shut up on Macy's whirling thoughts. The

Night Stalkers were the baddest helicopter pilots on the planet. She eased the collective up for the climb over Liga Pass. Tim wouldn't know that even on a calm day the winds aloft could still rip through the pass. Outside it was near perfect flying weather, the kind of day she always loved being aloft.

Baxter stuck his nose through the gap between the cockpit and main cabin over her shoulder and rested his muzzle there. She cooed in his ear and he let out a small contented noise.

"Emily had a kid with another Night Stalker. And the only reason Mark isn't more terrifying is because there's his wife to compare him to. He's our Incident Commander Air for all of Mount Hood Aviation, Emily is the lead pilot."

"And Jeannie?" she hated herself for asking.

"Jeannie..." Tim's voice sounded a little drifty.

Macy glanced over and decided she didn't like that look one bit. He was smiling in a way that—

"...is intense. She doesn't take crap from anybody. Hair about your color, with this wildfire red streak down the back. Flies like she's dancing across the sky. Jeannie and her husband—"

Okay, now Macy was feeling even stupider.

"—are the kind that you think are going to be the wild ones, but really they're two people used to being on their own. He's our photographer."

"You have your own photographer?"

Macy called the Ladd Airfield control tower at Fort Wainwright for clearance. She could feel Tim continuing to ride his hands on the controls, but letting her take the lead. It was an intimate connection, every little motion echoed, delayed by just an instant of backpressure on the controls.

"Jeannie married Cal Jackson."

"The *National Geographic* cover guy?"

"Yeah, that's him. If you saw his article on smokejumpers, Akbar and I are on one of the main spreads. Just our backs, but it's us."

She remembered the article. Had known it was Tim's outfit. She'd have to dig out the issue from under her bed and look at it again. How had she not recognized Tim?

"Where are we going anyway? Isn't this the Army base?"

Jeannie chatted with Jake in the control tower for a moment before entering the pattern and flying down to her usual spot by the service terminal.

"Weekly mail run," she rolled the throttle from Flight down to Idle, hit the release and rolled it to Off, then began shutting down the various systems.

The mail truck wasn't here yet—she checked her watch—nor would it be for another half hour.

"Be glad it isn't the monthly run. That's when I take the supplies out to the really remote villages. Makes for a long day. We're early. Why don't you let Baxter out?" For one thing, Baxter would want to stretch his legs. For another, she needed a little distance from Tim. He liked and respected the people he worked with, and they were among the best in the business. She'd never even met a Night Stalker and he flew with a pair of them? As a helicopter pilot she was having a bit of a fan-girl moment.

Tim had Baxter out, and the dog had dug out an old tennis ball from some corner of the passenger cabin. Tim began lofting it in high, effortless throws that sent the husky-lab mix galloping across the tarmac.

How in the hell was she supposed to survive a week of Tim being here? So close she could touch him, and so far away that he might as well be a character in...a magazine story.

She checked her watch again and cursed. Macy hadn't really expected Tim to come with her. She'd left early for her pickup to escape him. What the hell was she supposed to do with Tim Harada for half an hour?

CHAPTER 6

im followed Macy and Baxter as she led them east past the terminal building. He hung back a couple of steps to look around.

He'd never been to Ladd Airfield at Fort Wainwright. The Army base lay to the east of Fairbanks. He hadn't really been paying attention as they came into the pattern and landed. It was a single long airstrip that was quiet at the moment.

Some Army helicopters and a pair of jets to the west. Across the field were some small airplane hangers for general aviation. Overall it looked like a sleepy little place. A small twin-engine plane sailed almost silently down onto the runway as they walked along.

He also needed a little space from Macy. Even the way she walked was making his head hurt.

He'd felt her guiding his hands through the joined controls for the short flight—at a hundred and twenty miles an hour, the thirty of them had gone by too fast. It had been intimate, even sexy. Not just as if they were holding hands through the controls, but...

Argh!

Then, for a moment he'd swear she'd been jealous of Emily and Jeannie, but that made even less sense.

He was clearly losing his mind.

Why on Earth would he want to imagine Macy jealous of another woman? That it was Emily and Jeannie he'd imagined her reacting to only made him sure that he'd imagined it.

But even now, the slender woman, walking with perfect confidence beside this great dog that adored her…he couldn't look away. The sun was high enough that it glinted off her hair and made her shine, but left his footsteps walking in her still-long shadow.

His big chance.

If she were any other woman, it would have been his big chance to sweep her off her feet and have a quick tumble in Heinrich's barley.

Face it, Tim, Macy always confused the crap out of you. Even though she was four years younger, she'd always been three or four steps ahead of him. Just as she was now.

Enough of that.

He stretched out his stride and came up alongside her on Baxter's other side.

Of course now it felt as if they were walking as a couple. What would she do if he reached out and took her hand? What would he do? He'd held her hand plenty of times, back when they were kids and he was helping her back to her feet after her latest lame attempt to knock him down, or helping each other up off the Kung Fu mats. When she played sports, she played them for keeps.

Maybe he'd try it, just to see what it felt like. To see how she'd react. He prepared himself to be thrown down on the pavement just as they came around the terminal building. Then he spotted the two planes.

Two red-and-white painted Short Sherpa C-23s. The square-bodied, high-wing, twin-prop planes looked chunky and awkward. It was one of those planes that looked like it had been designed by a twelve-year old and could never fly. They were the backbone of any number of smokejumper teams. Each Sherpa could deliver ten smokies and two days of gear out the rear cargo hatch anywhere within three hundred miles of an airport.

He'd forgotten that the Bureau of Land Management Alaskan Fire Service smokejumpers were based here.

A couple guys were sorting gear out on the tarmac. One was…

"How you doing, Hank?" Tim gave it his best casual.

Hank Hammond jerked upright and looked at him in shock.

"Holy shit! Two-Tall Tim. How the hell are ya, buddy?" Hank hugged him and they traded back thumps. Hank was one of those guys who was burly with muscle and had a smile that looked like maybe dark corners were a good place to avoid—not wicked, just ready to tussle.

"You jumping with these guys?"

"Sure. Number two on the lead stick, I couldn't pass it up. The season up here is short, but intense as hell. What are you doing here?"

"Just visiting." Tim wasn't real excited with the way Hank eyed Macy who'd hung back a step. Then he reached out a hand and shook hers. "Woman like this standing beside me, I wouldn't just be visiting. How you doing, Macy? Damn but you're looking good today, girl."

"Just for you, Hank."

They knew each other. Of course they did. Tim's emotions were not only in chaos, they were also being stupid. Maybe he could get Macy to deliver some new ones as part of her mail run.

But they were flirting with each other which meant—*Doesn't mean squat, Harada.* He flirted with Jeannie all the time…though no one in their right mind flirted with Emily. Then why did it feel like…*Just let it go.*

"Did they put out a fire call to you, Macy? Why don't I know about it?" Hank was up on his toes, ready to sprint into action.

"No, just mail day. Running a bit early so I figured I drag Flame Boy here over to visit."

Hank eased back and nodded, taking a moment to shake off the leading edge of fire-call adrenaline.

"You still jumping with Akbar the Great?"

Tim nodded, "We're at Mount Hood Aviation now." That elicited a low, impressed whistle. "They gave us a rain break for a week. I grew up over in Larch Creek."

"Don't that beat all. Never pegged you for an man of the midnight sun. Yeah, I heard the Lower Forty-eight was socked in." Hank turned to Macy again, "Goofy looking pair, but the best damn stick I ever fought fire with. Learned a hell of a lot from those two down in Colorado and Utah. They're both just naturals, and that was before they got good."

Tim managed not to look at Macy, could feel the heat rising to his cheeks. The whole dynamic was different with a woman standing there.

No, it was a whole different dynamic with a woman *whose opinion he cared about* standing there.

Hank turned back to Tim. "Yeah, my girl's parents are up here in Fairbanks. Kid on the way, she wanted to be near home about the same time old Kent Thorpe retired and the slot came open, so we all win."

He had a girl and an incoming kid. Hank had been flirting with Macy the way Tim flirted with Jeannie; didn't mean a thing beyond friendly.

Clearly it was Tim's day to feel continually stupider and stupider. When you hit a day like that you could fight it or roll with it. Today he figured he was on vacation and should just roll with it. Fighting against the traces never worked anyway.

They hadn't fought fire together in three years, so they caught up on who they'd each jumped with and some of the fires.

He caught Macy looking at her watch.

"Looks like it's time for the mail, buddy. Can't be delaying that or they might arrest me. Great to see you."

"Give me your cell number, Tim." He shrugged at Tim's questioning look. "Never know if we might need you on a fire."

They shared a laugh, traded numbers, and he followed Macy and Baxter back to the helo.

"You guys were close," Macy asked as they strolled back through the warming air. He was beginning to regret choosing the heavy sweater over the too tight jacket. He pulled off the sweater and then repressed a shiver; it would be warm enough inside the helo. The airport was still quiet, not a lot of operations here early in the morning on a calm day.

"Close enough," he replied. "Hank Hammond is a good man to have at your back. Spent a season with him the same year I met Akbar. The four of us made an unstoppable team both on the fire and in the—"

"I get the picture," she cut him off.

Yep! Definitely a stupider-and-stupider day. How dumb would he be by nightfall? Especially considering that nightfall was still eighteen hours away and wouldn't be going much past twilight even when it arrived.

"Who was the fourth?" Macy gave him a subject change for which he was grateful.

"Axel Rodriguez. Died in a car wreck. He was always pushing the envelope. On the fire he was rock solid. But he was out in the world doing a hundred and forty plus when he lost control of his brand new Camaro. Empty road, broad daylight. Cops think he rolled it upward of ten times. Hell of a firefighter though."

"Sorry I asked."

Tim shook off the memory, "No problem. It was just one of those things. At least fire didn't get him."

AT LEAST FIRE *didn't get him.*

Macy wondered at that simple statement. Tim had changed in a lot more ways than she'd thought. He wasn't only in better shape, he'd faced death. Death of friends, death by fire.

Macy knew some folks who had died. The suicide rate in the roadless villages to the north was especially bad. She'd bring in a piece of mail, and a parent or friend would come forward to take it. She'd learned to recognize the solemnity marking that the recipient was no longer alive, and hand it over with as little reaction as possible.

Sometimes she'd haul a corpse off Denali, or as good as, because they were too far gone for even the medics to save. And each one of those unmet and often nameless losses hurt.

But none had been close to her; she knew she'd been lucky.

Tim had gone completely quiet as they walked back to the helo.

Juniper Willow was parked there, leaning against her U.S. Mail jeep, earbuds in, rocking out to her music player while she waited for them.

"What's on for today?" Macy shouted loud enough to be heard as she signed the register for the mail bag.

"Taylor Swift. She's so retro."

Macy managed not to laugh in Juniper's face. Juniper was maybe a year younger than Swift.

Juniper was gone by the time Macy had the mail bag and Baxter in the back of the LongRanger.

Tim still looked numb; hurt by the memories she'd stirred up.

She stepped up and rested a hand on his chest in apology.

And then, like a miracle, as if it was the most natural thing on the planet, he folded her into his arms and pulled her against him.

Macy didn't freeze in surprise this time. She let herself flow against him; one arm trapped between them, the other around his waist that she used to pull herself against him. He was not supposed to feel better than her imagination, but he did. He was real, alive, and—for this one moment—in her arms.

She laid her head on his shoulder and he buried his face in her hair.

They stood like that for a moment that she knew she'd cherish as if it had lasted a gazillion hours rather than just a few seconds.

Then he whispered in her ear as if speaking to himself, "Missed you, Mace."

He shifted back a half step and banged up against the passenger side door he'd left open.

"Sorry," he cleared his throat. "Shouldn't have done that. I just..." His voice petered out.

Her hand still rested on his chest. She could feel his heart racing, but she didn't think it was passion by the look in his eyes. They were closed, tight and hard against memories.

She slid her hand up behind his neck and pulled her down to him. It was meant to be a friendly kiss, sympathy and no more.

It started there, just the merest brush of lips.

Then his hands were back around her and he hauled her against him. She'd never kissed Tim before, not even a kid's practice kiss, but this was something else he was really good at. Really good.

Macy leaned into it until he was pinned against the side of the LongRanger. She dug her hands into his hair to keep him there, to keep him from evaporating back into her dreams. With those big powerful hands, he clamped onto her; one scooped into her hair and the other wrapped around her waist so hard she could barely breathe.

Didn't want to breathe.

Just wanted to—

Baxter let out a yip from behind the window to the passenger cabin.

And just that fast, the moment was gone.

One moment Tim had been giving her the most amazing kiss ever and the next she was two steps back with his hands planted firmly about her waist.

"Shit, I'm sorry, Mace."

She hit him. A hard punch to the gut that he wasn't tensed up for this time.

MACY HADN'T FORGOTTEN any of her training.

Tim tried to wheeze in a breath, but his spasming stomach muscles wouldn't have anything to do with it yet. He managed little gulps that sounded like backward hiccups.

Macy was livid as she stomped away. When she turned to stomp back, he knew he'd never seen her so angry. For an instant he regretted all of those Kung Fu classes they'd done together.

She stormed right up to him and shouted at point blank range.

"Are you really that stupid?"

"It's my," he managed another tiny gulp, "Stu-pid Day. So. Yes. I am." He hadn't crossed one line, he'd crossed a hundred. He didn't know what had come over him. He'd never before kissed a woman without permission. He'd certainly never used his strength to overpower someone.

But the smell of Macy Tyler's hair had been his undoing. Her intensely fit body had molded against his in ways that had lit fires inside his own. And her hand resting so lightly on his chest...

"Won't. Happen again," he managed four syllables on the last breath.

She stared at him in shock, and then she did the damnedest thing. She clamped her hands on either side of his head, pulled him down to her, and kissed him hard.

Angry hard.

Full of need hard.

So hard that it filled his head with images that suggested maybe he should have dragged her off into Heinrich's fields.

So hard that it went soft, pliant, and warm until at some indefinable moment they shifted from kissing to simply lying against each other wrapped tight in each other's arms. She lay against him, he lay against the helicopter, and Baxter offered sharp barks of frustration mostly muffled by the Plexiglas, but very close to his head based on the thumping he could feel against the back of his skull.

Macy's head was on his shoulder. His face was in her hair.

His arms were holding her.

Macy.

This was so not right...but it was right in so many ways.

He raised a hand from her back to glance at his watch.

Six-thirty a.m. He'd been awake for three hours.

How had so much changed in three hours? He needed some time to absorb all this.

"Guessing it's time to go deliver the mail."

Without moving out of his arms, she pulled back enough to look at his face for a long moment.

Then she closed her eyes on an exasperated sigh and began beating her forehead against his shoulder just as she had knocked it against the breakfast table this morning.

CHAPTER 7

Macy could still feel that kiss as she lifted the LongRanger from the Ladd Airfield runway and turned northwest to begin her standard loop that she'd dubbed the Great Village Circle Route, because it ended at the town of Circle on the Yukon River.

It started at Stevens Village, which with a population of eighty-seven was the largest of her stops. Stevens was twenty miles from the nearest road and sixty northwest of Fairbanks. After that she'd travel generally eastward stopping at over a dozen roadless villages until she was northeast of Fairbanks at Circle, which had been isolated all summer due to a shift in the Yukon River that had erased the only road access.

Her lips were sore from the power of Tim's, her head was spinning...and Baxter sat happily on the copilot's seat beside her looking out at the sunny summer day and the green forests rolling by below, interrupted only by glittering lines of the Yukon River and its tributaries.

She was still trying to piece together quite how that had happened.

Tim had delivered the all-time, history-making, dumbest, post-amazing-kiss line.

Ever.

Then he had opened his mouth to say something that was bound to be even stupider, if possible, when feet came pounding up behind her.

"Tim!" It had been Hank Hammond. "You're still here. Great! I can't find Tony anywhere and we've got a call. Please say you'll jump with me. It's a hot one deep in the ANWR. We've got to stop it before it gets down to Arctic Village."

Arctic Village was about the farthest out village anywhere in Alaska. A fire could burn almost anywhere in the massive Alaska National Wildlife Refuge and affect only wildlife, and not much of that. By pure chance a wildfire was threatening the only small community for a hundred miles around.

Tim had at least had the presence of mind to look at her in confusion.

"I...We..." he stuttered like an airplane piston engine with a failing magneto.

"...need to..."

"...talk...."

"...don't we?"

At least he got that much right.

"Come on, man," Hank pleaded. "Tony's our lead, I'm second-man on his stick, not a lead. I need the Two-Tall Harada magic."

Macy had thumped her forehead against Tim's shoulder one final time in frustration and then given him a hard shove that sent him stumbling in Hank's direction.

Then he'd done the goofiest thing. He'd moved back to her and brushed his fingertips from her temple to her jaw, kissed her on the forehead, and then sprinted toward the smokejumper hangars. He'd called back for Macy to tell his mom he'd be fine.

She didn't even remember letting Baxter move to the front, or taking off and heading north. She could only hope that she'd cleared properly with the tower.

Macy was climbing out of Stevens when her second radio, that she'd tuned to the Bureau of Land Management fire frequency, crackled to life.

She'd been hoping for a call for her services, she could be there in a couple hours, or could have been. If she was called now, she'd have to double back to Larch Creek for equipment, refuel in Fairbanks, and then fly two hours north. But no call came in.

The transmission was from the Sherpa which had taken an hour to even reach the fire because Arctic Village was so near the edge of the map even by Alaskan standards.

"We've got two hundred acres involved, spreading before a thirty-knot wind." Despite the crackle of radio signal breaking up across the three hundred miles that separated them, she recognized that it was Tim's voice reporting, not Hank's.

He sounded different as he called out a plan to the two SEATs— Single Engine Air Tankers—that were following the Sherpa jump planes northward. This wasn't Timothy Harada—her sorta older brother. It was completely the man who had just kissed her silly. This was Two-Tall Tim, premier smokejumper. His low voice was deeper, clearer despite the distance.

All that uncertainty that he'd been displaying around her all morning was gone. No awkward stammers. No allusions to it being a Stupid Day whatever he'd meant by that.

He called out jump coordinates and multiple attack vectors the way she'd call out a lunch order at French Pete's, as if it was all second nature.

She overflew the next village and had to circle back several miles.

Well, that kiss hadn't been second nature for either of them. Maybe she should cut Tim some slack. Macy had imagined kissing him since she'd decided kissing anybody could possibly be a good thing.

Of course she'd come to the idea probably later than most. She'd read one of her mom's books with an aliens-having-sex scene when she was nine and been so weirded out by imagining her mother writing a sex scene that she hadn't recovered for a long time afterward.

And by the time she'd warmed up to the idea, she'd been in junior high and Tim had been a high school junior dating Sally Kirkman. It would have helped if Sally had been more unlikable, or less well endowed.

Then he'd gone Lower Forty-eight for school. Somehow her fifteen-year-old brain hadn't caught up with quite what that meant until he was gone. Even that first summer, when anyone else would have come home, he was working wildfires and only made it back once for two days.

"The way I see it," she told Baxter as she lifted out of Alatna and headed for Allakaket—the two towns separated by a couple hundred meters of muddy river. "Tim gets one 'Get Out of Dork-Jail Free' card. He'd better de-Dork by the time he gets back from this fire."

And a sudden rage swept through her, so badly that her hand was shaking on the cyclic as she struggled to land at Allakaket. He was here a week at most—that was all she'd have him for before he returned to Oregon and his easy-women-filled life. One week, and he was off jumping a fire over Arctic Village for who knew how many days.

God damn it. When did life start being fair?

TIM HAD TRIED several times to take a background role, but Hank wasn't having anything to do with it.

"I was always a Number Two man, you know that."

He did, but he hadn't realized that Hank did. He had good fire instincts, knew how to read a burn, and wasn't afraid of it. Give him even a hint of a plan and he could implement it with style.

But the lead smokie had to be so much more than that. The Number One slot was the leader of a Type I Incident Response Team like smokejumpers. Tim and Akbar had even gone through the additional training together to make it to Type III Incident Commanders —not just team leaders. Earthquake, flood, hurricane...it didn't matter; they had specific training on how to find a solution and make it happen.

So, Tim had kept Hank in the loop, but stepped up into the lead slot. He didn't know the burn rate of the sparse trees and grassland this far north, but Hank did. Was he looking at deep bog or a thin layer of growth over a hard layer of permafrost? The latter. Thin enough to clear easily down to mineral soils that wouldn't burn? Not a chance.

Between them, they knocked together a plan of attack and to the letter of Tim's instructions, the Sherpa pilot dropped them and their gear right on target.

As soon as he was down and had his parachute stowed, he walked up to a forty-foot pine, one of the larger ones, and tried to snap a one-inch branch. It should crackle, complain, bend and recover.

With a sharp crack, it folded in half and only a small stringer of bark held it in place at all. Dry as a bone.

He showed it to Hank who swore. "No way it should be that dry in mid-July."

Tim surveyed the terrain. This wasn't a wildfire rolling through sparse woods. This was a blaze in a tinder box.

The rest of the crew was jumping in while he was formulating a final plan of attack. He wished Akbar was here to run it by. He wished Henderson was circling his Incident Commander Air plane overhead with his daughter giggling in the passenger seat.

Alaska Fire Service ran a smaller crew than most jump outfits— when it got bad, the Missoula smokies would fly up to lend a hand. Twenty-one of twenty-two jumpers had made it to the planes…still no word on Tony. MHA had that many, and another twenty-man Hot Shot team. Local fire service was almost always around to help if there was a logging road even close. The nearest road to Arctic Village was a couple of parallel creases in the permafrost that they'd over-flown a hundred miles ago.

Instead of the MHA complement of two Firehawks and three MD500s in addition to any fixed wing planes the US Forest Service might be sending in, he only had two SEATs which would be here in an hour to scoop river water and dump it on the fire. Each Single-

Engine Air Tanker could carry about three-quarters as much as a Firehawk could deliver.

It was all he had and he'd have to make do.

All *he* had.

The fire was his!

He'd never commanded a whole fire before. Even on the small ones, it had been his and Akbar's. He could hardly wait for a chance to rub this fire in Akbar's face. While his friend was all down and snuggly with his amazing new wife, Tim would be leading his first fire.

Leading his first fire, he acknowledged, and wondering what the heck to do with the woman who was waiting for him.

Would it be with another kiss like one he'd never had in his life... or would it be a busted snout like the one she'd given to Billy Wilkins?

He'd have to worry about that later.

The Sherpa C-23s made a final pass dropping a pallet of pumps, hose, spare fuel, and food. They were in it now.

He gave Hank a five-man team and the impossible task of getting the pumps into nearby streams and pools, and soaking the underbrush; there weren't the resources to clear it.

Tim took the rest of the team and began dropping trees, chopping them up, and dragging them downwind. Swamping all those branches was hard work, especially shoving through thick underbrush, but he couldn't leave them where they'd let the fire catch and burn.

They needed a firebreak a hundred feet wide, a mile-and-a-half long, and, at the fire's current rate of approach, they needed it before midnight.

CHAPTER 8

*M*acy sat at the bar in French Pete's and did her best to ignore the ongoing silence from her portable radio. She'd already called the BLM post clerk at Ladd Airfield twice on her cell phone.

"Your boy doesn't waste a whole lot of words on the air," he'd told her. "But he thinks he'll contain it sometime overnight without calling up any additional support. Hank Hammond says to trust him and I rang his boss down at Mount Hood Aviation. A Mark Henderson said that Tim is almost as good at reading a fire as their dedicated Fire Behavior Analyst. 'Course I knew he was lying through his teeth, they've got the Fire Witch reading fires for them. Still, it's high praise."

And Macy had to accept it whether or not she wanted to. Without a call-up, no one was going to pay her expenses up to the fire and once she got there, she wouldn't be authorized to fight the fire anyway.

Macy had the *National Geographic* folded up in her back pocket, the one with Tim and Akbar's photo in it. No wonder she hadn't recognized them, two tiny men staring up at a two-page spread of roaring inferno. But their presence totally made the image, showing the overwhelming scale they faced and battled. And Tim really was two

Akbars tall. Even in their tiny corner of the photo, their height discrepancy was dramatic.

The article had also talked about the "Fire Witch," the best FBAN working the West Coast fires. She was the fire analyst who'd beaten the New Tillamook Burn.

"You're not playing very well."

Macy blinked and looked down at the chess board on Carl's bar, up at Natalie, then back down at the board. She had been playing, hadn't she?

According to the positioning of the pieces on the board, she wouldn't be beating any ten-year olds today.

"Sorry, Short Stuff."

"Do you *have* to keep calling me that?" Natty wiped out one of Macy's bishops. The other one was...already taken. Crap. She liked bishops—they were sly and sneaky, doing strange attacks at odd angles.

"Have to. It's the law. I gotta do it while I can. You're already taller than I was at your age, and way prettier." Macy struck back with a mighty pawn move that, in retrospect, achieved nothing but put her one step closer to defeat.

"I'm pretty?" Natty looked up in surprise.

"Gorgeous," Macy's dad came up and kissed Natty on top the bright blond curls that shone even in French Pete's dim interior.

"You too," and he kissed Macy on the forehead.

"Biased," she told him as she did every time he said something like that.

"Absolutely. You're my gal."

Natty finished cremating Macy's pieces before Carl could even finish drawing a beer for her dad.

"Maybe I'll do some homework," then she shot a wicked grin at Macy, "I mean algebra has to be harder than beating you, doesn't it?"

"Next time, Short Stuff."

"Not for much longer, Stick Girl."

"That Ms. Stick Girl to you."

They stuck out their tongues at each other, but Macy had to work to find the smile. If Natalie took after her mom, she'd end up pretty in more than just her hair and face. Whereas the nicest thing that could be said about her own figure was "sleek." "Stick Girl" would have been an apt nickname, as much now as back in high school, if she hadn't gained a reputation early on for beating the crap out of anyone who used it.

She followed her father over to one of the booths, the one she'd been in with Tim just this morning. Then, when Natalie called to her, Macy had to double back to fetch her painfully silent radio and barely touched Coke.

"What has you so snarled up, sweetheart? Anything bad happen with Brett?"

"What? Brett?" What was he doing in this conversation? Oh, last night's date. "Oh, no. He was fine."

"It was good to see you dating again."

"It wasn't—" she gave it up. "Okay, it was, but it wasn't. I aimed him at Linda Lee."

"Always wondered why they didn't get together."

Macy had long ago learned that her dad saw far more than was comfortable.

"It's from spending so much time with your mom," he'd explain every time she whined about it. Josh Tyler saw who was pairing up and who was breaking up in Macy's high school years, usually weeks before she did. Of course, he'd been everyone's favorite teacher—he'd totally rocked third grade, even for her once she got over the stigma of being the teacher's kid—so that probably gave him an inside track.

Once, when she'd been much younger, he'd made the mistake of pointing out some things about Tim Harada and Sally Kirkman, and then they'd gotten together; the hot item for all four years of high school. She hadn't talked to her father for months after that. Ever since, Tim, Stephen, and her own relationships had been strictly off-limits between them.

"Did you see him this morning?"

"You're doing it again, Dad," she sighed. No need to ask who "him" was. Macy was twenty-five and still fighting a lost cause. Fine, there were only so many fronts she could be contrary on at once. "Yeah, I did. We spent a couple hours together."

"Where is he? I haven't seen him since last night."

"Arctic Village."

He looked at her in surprise.

"Fighting a forest fire." On his vacation, rather than spending time with her…no, she wasn't going to think about what they'd be doing if they were together. Partly because she hadn't a clue; fighting or— And she definitely wasn't going to think about *that* in front of her father.

"You don't want me to say it, so I won't."

"Grown women are not supposed to be so transparent to their fathers."

"It's only because I love you so much, sweetheart."

Macy sighed, glared at her silent radio for putting her in this predicament.

Her father sat silently.

"Say it."

Now it was her father's turn to study his beer, shift it around in little twists until he'd turned it through a full three-sixty.

"Go on!" Macy clamped her tongue in her teeth against the tone. Her father smiled rather than being put off.

"You two always had something special together."

"Yeah, I kept dragging him into trouble and he kept me from getting in too deep."

Her father nodded, then sipped his beer. "Yep. That's about right. He always did love you."

She was still gaping at him when Mom slid in beside him.

"I killed him gloriously," she crowed as she waved at Carl for a pint.

"You killed the hero?" Then that smile of his started. "Does he get resurrected later in the book?"

"Not a chance, Mister. His ass was vaporized, across six dimensions and three timelines," she kissed her husband on the cheek. "Besides, I never agreed he was the hero of this story."

Macy closed her eyes and tried not to think about the man facing a fire three hundred miles over the horizon.

———

THERE WERE times that night that Tim wished he'd called up more air support. The fire had dodged south before turning east once more. It would have been a good time to have another plane or chopper on site.

When the BLM clerk had informed him that the nearest asset was three hours out, Tim had declined. Three hours from now they'd have either beaten the beast or they would be in full retreat.

They had to drive the fire break another half mile out. A dozen villagers had arrived over the rough terrain on four-wheel ATVs. He got them shifting equipment and making sure his team was kept supplied with water, food, and fuel for their saws and pumps.

Three hours.

That's about how fast Macy and her LongRanger could be here from Larch Creek. *Right.* That was probably the asset that the post clerk had been referring to.

Too late now.

He hoped she wasn't taking it personally. MHA had enough rockin' female heli-pilots that any bias he'd had about women in harm's way had long since been extinguished. Besides Krista bucked fire just as effectively as he and Akbar did when the three of them jumped a fire together.

He could really use the two of them right now.

"Hank!" he grabbed the man by his harness and they leaned on each other for support.

After sixteen hours on the fire, the only thing that kept them upright was being in constant motion so that they didn't simply tip over sideways. Stopping led perilously close to the danger of simply collapsing to the soil in exhaustion.

"Cut me a hole, Hank. That line, right there," he held out an arm. "Take your best sawyer and make a path even twenty feet wide. In ten minutes I'll send another team to take the next twenty feet and so on. We're going to open up the line in a wedge form, but your goal is get me even twenty feet of breathing room all the way across in front of the fire. Don't look back, because if you do, we'll run over your lazy behind."

Too exhausted to speak, Hank punched his acknowledgement against Tim's shoulder and took off shouting for Tina. Tina? Tim didn't even know he had a woman on the crew. They were common enough among the Hot Shots now, but female smokies were few and far between.

"Go get 'em!" he croaked after the pair as they began slicing into the tree line. Tim rubbed at his shoulder.

It wasn't that Hank's punch had hurt, but he'd hit right where Macy's head had rested against his shoulder after they'd kissed. Somewhere in the firefight, he'd come to terms with that. He still had no idea at all of what to do about it, but he wasn't going to be complaining if she was willing to try it again.

MACY HADN'T SLEPT a single blink all night. She'd even let Baxter up on the foot of the bed, which always made him so happy that it was like going to sleep bathed in the dog's joy.

Not a single eye blink.

After breakfast—she still needed to get milk and eggs—knowing she was a complete idiot, she drove down to the hangar and pulled out the LongRanger.

Screw the expense! She was going to fly up to Arctic Village on her own dime.

Macy dragged the folded up Bambi fire-fighting bucket to the bird and leveraged it into the cabin...just in case. When in use, the big orange bucket dangled a hundred feet below her helo and could scoop up two hundred gallons in seconds. It took up two seats, but it was worth bringing it along.

She was passing Fairbanks and striking north when her radio

squawked.

"Ladd Airfield smokie to Tyler. You out there, Macy?"

It was Hank. The fear hit her like a slap. Why would Hank be calling her? Where was Tim?

"Here!" she managed in a desperate gasp.

"Easy, girl," he chuckled. "Didn't mean to spook you. I got a passed out piece of meat here with your name on it. You want me to hold it for pick up or stuff it into a handy bunk?"

Macy slammed over the controls hard enough for Baxter to yip in surprise as he scrambled for purchase on the copilot's seat.

"I'll..." *take a deep breath.* That seemed to help so she took another and then wondered if she was about to hyperventilate and pass out with relief. She really needed to teach Baxter how to fly just in case. "...fetch him now. Why don't you just prop him up outside for me. I'll drop a longline and haul him home." There, that sounded more normal.

She hit the other radio and called the control tower for permission to enter the pattern.

"Will do, Macy," Hank's knowing chuckle was cut off when he released his transmit key.

Less than two minutes later she was idling down the engine and looking at Tim slumped against the side of one of the Sherpas. Hank had helped Tim to his feet by the time she reached them.

"Hey, Mace," Tim brightened up as she took his other arm. He leaned in and placed a sloppy kiss on her cheek. He reeked of smoke and char. His face was blackened with soot as was the Nomex gear that was still draped over him.

But he was having real trouble placing one foot in front of the other.

"Are you hurt?"

"Nah!" Hank answered for him as Tim stumbled back toward the helo. "Turns out he'd just come off a ten-day burn down in California before he came up here. Wouldn't have known it yesterday and last night though. Damn! I was sure that was a two-day fire, maybe three. With Tim out in front the whole way, we beat it in one."

There was no way to get him into the copilot's seat. Tim's long legs, heavy fire gear, and complete lack of motor control defeated their best efforts to get him into the seat. She finally opened the rear cabin door and tipped him over onto the floor. He was asleep before he hit the deck.

They closed him in and stood outside for a moment beneath the slowly whirling rotor blades.

"Thanks, Hank."

"You bet. You were here pretty damn quick."

"Happened to be passing nearby..." she didn't know what to say to him.

"With a two hundred gallon Bambi bucket stowed in your passenger cabin. Got the picture. Seriously, Macy. I've been jumping fire for over five years. I knew he and Akbar were the best; I just never really understood what that meant 'til now."

"Go home, Hank. Go see your lady." She kissed his cheek in thanks, which was such a girly gesture that it totally surprised her even if Hank just took it in stride.

"You see to your man, Macy. He's a good one." And Hank was moving back toward the hangar not all that much steadier on his feet than Tim had been. Tim wasn't the only good man who'd been on that fire.

She was aloft in minutes, flying as smoothly as she could, though nothing short of another fire would probably wake him.

It wasn't until Macy was halfway back to Larch Creek that Hank's words sank in.

Her man?

When the hell had that happened?

———

MACY WASN'T QUITE sure why she'd done it the way she had. Maybe it was that the only way she'd found to move Tim was to back her pickup right up against the passenger cabin opening and drag him across like a sack of coffee beans.

At the time it had struck her as an ignominious way to deliver him back it his parents. *Hi! Here's your exhausted, dirty, smelly son. Good luck with him.*

Instead she'd taken him back to her place, driving around to the back kitchen door and getting the tailgate over the rear porch. Then she'd looked at him. Her own hands and arms were already black-smeared from handling him.

"Well, Harada. This is gonna be a new experience for both of us."

She stripped off his borrowed boots and smoke gear right there in the truck bed. Next were the cotton long johns that were also black at collar, wrists, and ankles.

Macy had him most of the way out of them before she really thought about what he'd be wearing underneath. It turned out to be a white cotton tank top and blue briefs, briefs being the operative word. Couldn't the man at least have worn boxers under there? These left far too little to the imagination.

Especially since she didn't know if he was thinking their kiss before the fire had been serious or an invitation to a fling.

And neither did she.

"Well, Tyler. You're the one who caught this fish and fetched it home. What are you going to do with it now?"

Finish the job.

She started with a washcloth and a bucket of soapy water. He was only sooty from the neck up and the wrists out, so she'd just concentrate on those. When gentle brushes failed to produce much result she began scrubbing, finally in earnest.

He roused enough to blink at her in protest, then smiled.

"Macy," he sounded very pleased as one of his hands moved to cup her breast.

The shock was enough to steal her breath in that moment before he passed out once more. She peeled his hand off her breast. It was the first time she'd heard him say her proper name since they'd been kids and that took her breath away as much as the grope. *Mace* was a kid, a nickname that felt as if it was adding distance every time Tim used it.

Macy was who she had grown up to be and at least his near-unconscious mind acknowledged that.

Macy returned to washing his face.

"Yep!" she tried to make her voice Neanderthal low as she spoke to Baxter who had perched on the back porch to oversee the operation. "I dragged it home, gonna clean it up and then..." she had no idea what.

"Stupid Day! Ha!" she told Baxter. "I get it. Yesterday everything Tim did was *stupid*. Today must be my turn."

Baxter wasn't arguing.

Well if it *was* her Stupid Day then there was no way she would finish this without being totally embarrassed. She finished his hands and had returned to cleaning Tim's face when she heard her name called from out front.

"Out back," she shouted and sighed. Resigned, she focused on cleaning one of his ears.

"Hi, Macy. Have you seen my son?" Eva Harada was already speaking as she came around the corner of the house. She didn't have the decency to look shocked, surprised, or even a little alarmed when she took in the scene. Instead a smile lit her face as she stepped over the smokejumper gear that Macy had jettisoned over the side and looked into the truck bed at her prostrate son.

"Hi, Eva. Yes, it seems I have."

"I see that. Have you noticed that he always looks like he's up to something when he's asleep? Most children look more innocent asleep than awake, but Tim was always backwards about that. Used to scare me to death as a mother. I was always worried that he would grow into that look."

Macy stared down at him. She'd never thought about it, but could see it now. Had noticed it before too, like the time she'd snuck into the Harada's house to slide a shovelful of snow under Tim's blankets. He had looked so dangerous that she'd almost snuck off deed undone. But ultimately she'd decided it was only all the more reason to follow through.

Then she thought of the electric kiss yesterday, and the way he'd just smiled while groping her breast.

"Maybe he is growing into it."

Eva hummed in the back of her throat, "Would you like some help?"

"Well, I think this is about as clean as I'm going to get him without tossing him in the river. Let me get a blanket over him and I can bring him home for you."

Eva smiled up at her.

"What?" And then she knew. "Not you too?"

"Me *too?*" Eva did her best to look all innocent and Macy could see exactly where Tim had gotten his present sly and sneaky expression.

"My father."

"Josh Tyler was always a smart man," Eva looked back down into the truck bed. "Tim is right where he should be. I'll help you get him inside."

And that easily, the two of them were moving Tim—a man she'd only kissed for the first time yesterday—into her bed with only a minimum of his help. He collapsed into it with a sigh, buried his face in her pillow, and settled back into sleep.

Without a word, Eva pulled Macy down and kissed her on both cheeks before leaving. As Macy was pulling the blackout curtains around her bedroom, Eva was crossing back around the house, wiping at her eyes.

She was crying? But she hadn't looked sad.

Definitely Macy's turn for a Stupid Day. Eva Harada was crying and smiling at the same time because she believed something that wasn't true. They weren't lovers; they didn't have a future. All they had was a kiss.

Why was Macy the only one who could see that?

She finished darkening the bedroom and headed back out to her truck to clean up the mess. She was almost done when her father came up. At least there was nothing to be embarrassed about now.

"He make it back okay?"

Macy considered being frustrated that again there was no need to define who "he" was, but decided it wasn't worth the effort.

"Yeah! Eva Harada helped me shove him into bed."

There. That made it sound all respectable and on the up and up. She'd just ignore the fact that she was holding Tim's long johns at the moment. She rolled them up as nonchalantly as she could.

"Out on his feet," she continued, not overly quickly. It came out sounding right. "According to Hank Hammond, Tim has only slept about a dozen hours in the last twelve days. Turns out he just came off a big fire in the Lower Forty-eight."

"Cottonwood Peak. That was a bad one." Why was her father more informed about what Tim was doing than she was? She should be the one who knew what her...

Shit! She didn't have a word for Tim anymore. Friend? Not after that kiss. Lover? Not that either. Or at least not yet. She liked the way that thought sounded though.

"You need anything?"

"Milk and eggs, but I'll deal with that as soon as I clean this up."

"Okay," he leaned over and kissed her cheek before heading back around the house. "You may want to change your shirt before you go into town," and he was gone.

Macy looked down.

A very large, sooty handprint was perfectly imprinted over the right breast of her white I (heart) My Helo t-shirt. A handprint that had been there the whole time her father had been talking to her...and Tim's mom as well.

She closed her eyes and waited. Yep! No question at all. This was definitely her Stupid Day.

TIM HAD BEEN out for twelve hours straight by the time Macy finally wound down.

She'd changed, washed her truck, gone grocery shopping, and done a load of laundry, both his and hers together—which had been surprisingly intimate. Lack of sleep last night finally caught up with her at about the same time as a total lack of common sense.

Macy came to on her feet, leaning against the door jamb of her own bedroom and looking down at the man asleep in her bed. She didn't want to sleep on the couch, she always woke with a severe kink in her neck if she fell asleep while watching a movie or reading there.

Here she had a perfectly comfortable queen size bed with a beautiful man curled up in it.

Stupid Day.

By paying strict attention, she hadn't done anything stupid since her father had left. Well, other than immediately stripping off the offending t-shirt the moment before her neighbor Jack Jamison had pulled his truck around the back, next door. At least she'd been wearing a bra, even if it had been a frilly black one rather than her usual white cotton. She wasn't even sure how she'd come to be wearing it—this wasn't her normal fare.

Now, the last daylight was wandering in the living room window, poking down the hall, and spilling softly through the door and over Tim's sleeping form.

Stupid Day.

Thinking it over, there was one moment that hadn't been stupid.

It had been strangely perfect.

Too exhausted to function, definitely incoherent, he had groped her breast. And while doing it, despite his condition, he'd said her name.

Not the nickname he had used every single time since he'd tagged her with it, but her own name. And it had sounded wonderful.

She decided to take courage from those two simple syllables.

Macy pulled off her t-shirt, the plain bra she'd switched to after a shower, jeans and matching underwear. She folded it all on the top of her bedroom dresser, took one last look at Tim to gather her nerves, and closed the door behind her.

In pitch darkness she slid in beside him.

After all, if a girl was going to be stupid, she should really go for it.

She could hear Baxter curl up on his bed just inside the door.

Much to her surprise, she fell asleep easily.

CHAPTER 9

*J*im *woke in pitch* darkness.

Post fire. He knew the feeling, every muscle ready to complain if he moved unexpectedly; partly the workout of a fire, partly from sleeping in one position for a massive number of hours. Also, his body had that floating feeling of being desperate for calories.

But he didn't usually wake from a fire with his arm around a woman's waist. That came later, or used to anyway.

Nor was there any of the normal question about who was in bed with him, nobody on the planet felt or smelled like Macy Tyler. He just wasn't sure how he'd come *to be* in bed with her. His mattress and sheets didn't feel like his. That meant he was in her bed.

But the woman felt—well, now that he'd admitted to himself how much he'd enjoyed kissing Macy, it was safe to admit—incredible. In their sleep they'd spooned together, his other arm beneath her pillowed head, his face buried in her hair. That would explain the good dreams. He didn't actually remember them, but it was impossible to have any other type in their current position.

For a moment he wondered if it was okay that he was here, and then the rest of his brain woke up. He hadn't been in any condition to care where he'd slept, or have any say in it that he'd remembered. It was her choice to be here beside him.

He had a leftover Stupid Day thought that he should let her sleep. But no, that day was behind him now. He wasn't going to think about yesterday or tomorrow. He was going to think about the woman in his arms.

Tim began moving his hand over her, belly, hip, thigh, hip, waist, up to her arm. She wasn't only here with him, she wasn't wearing anything; neither nightgown nor t-shirt.

She had made him an offer, made by a childhood friend grown to a beautiful woman, to choose whether to accept or reject.

He dug his nose into her hair again and breathed her in.

That choice didn't even count as one of Macy Tyler's trick questions.

MACY COULD PRACTICALLY HEAR Tim thinking. She'd woken the instant his breathing changed, trying not to change her own breathing as he woke slowly and reacted to the choices she'd made for him.

That single long tantalizing stroke of his hand down and back up her body had been electric. His hands were callus-rough and Tim-gentle; even with such a simple gesture, no one had ever touched her quite like that. It felt as if he wasn't just appreciating a female form, but the woman inside as well. Her.

She knew his choice the moment he buried his face in her hair and she wanted to get up and do a happy dance.

And a case of jitters slammed in with it. What had she done? This was Tim Harada. Her closest childhood friend, her romantic hero from every girlhood fancy, and in town for only five more days. How long had they slept? It might even be four days by now.

Don't think, Macy! Don't think! The orders didn't do much good. Her stupid brain wouldn't shut up. She didn't want a one-night stand, nor a four-night one. And she didn't want a long-distance relation-ship. She wanted to come home and find Tim waiting for her and—

she was a hopeless dork. They didn't have a relationship. They didn't...

Tim stroked his hand once again over her bare midriff.

She should have worn a t-shirt.

His fingers trailed up her hip.

A t-shirt that reached her knees.

Down her thigh and returned just as slowly.

And sweatpants. And armor. And been in a different bed. In a different country. On another planet in another—

"Shh," Tim's soft whisper as he reached up to stroke her hair sent a wave of quiet over her racing thoughts as if he in turn could feel her thinking.

Macy tried to breathe, with very little luck; it caught hard in her throat.

"You sure, Mace?"

She was here, wasn't she? Which meant she'd been sure at some point even if she wasn't now. Since she was a total train wreck at the moment, she'd trust to her earlier decision. Unable to speak, she nodded.

Again he began his slow inspection, his hand sliding up between her breasts, brushing her cheek, tracing the edge of her breast only on its downward journey.

Everywhere his hand traveled, it was as if those rough calluses were peeling off a thin layer that had existed beyond her skin. A layer that, when removed by this touch, left her more exposed than any mere removal of clothes. It was...cleansing. As if Tim's touch stripped away layer after layer of the uncertain girl and revealed more and more of the confident woman she had spent her life trying to be.

You are confident, she told herself. And with each newly stroked nerve ending sighing with contentment, it became more true. She rolled just enough to press deeper into the spoon against him, and hook a leg backward over his.

He seemed so fascinated by her hip. She rested a hand over his, not to guide, just to follow his exploration.

"Not a lot of curves on this girl," she confessed.

"The curves don't make the woman," he whispered then finally scooped her breast to nestle in his palm. "These are some very nice curves you have, Miss Tyler."

"But they certainly aren't Sally Kirkman-esque."

Tim stopped fondling her for a moment, then huffed out a breath of surprise. "Wow! Haven't thought about her in a while. Any idea what she's up to?"

Macy considered the angle of attack of her elbow on Tim's gut, but it wouldn't be as hard a blow as she'd like to deliver.

"What?"

"First," she managed through gritted teeth, "it's rude as hell to discuss one woman while you're fondling another. Second, you were in love with her all through high school and you don't know what she's doing?"

Tim bit her lightly on the shoulder.

Macy did her best not to take any pleasure from it and failed miserably.

"Second, we weren't in love. And, first, I'm not the one who brought her up."

Macy tried to struggle free.

All her wriggling achieved was to roll her over until she was face-to-face with Tim and the hand that had been cradling her breast was now scooped over her butt, but kept her just as firmly anchored in place. She wished she could see him, but the blackout curtains were still in place.

"Would you care to explain how you can be lovers for four straight years and not be in love?"

"Easy, we weren't lovers. At least not for most of it."

There had to be more offensive men than Tim Harada, but at the moment she couldn't think of one.

"Sally bloomed early," Tim sounded as if he was talking about the weather.

"Yeah. Hard to miss that," she'd been the envy of every single girl in school.

"Nobody missed that. Nobody in our classes, nor her brothers or father." Tim's low voice took on a growl that spoke of exactly what kind of attention she'd been receiving.

Macy felt a cold chill and shivered. Tim ran a hand over her back and it only left her colder.

"I was bigger than any of them, and with Mom's martial arts training since I could walk, I was also more dangerous."

Macy could barely whisper, "What did you do?"

"You want to hear this?"

She could only nod.

Tim took a deep breath before continuing. "I threatened to break one bone in all three of their bodies for each time any of them even touched Sally. That took care of the family anyway. The way I protected her in school was I became her boyfriend. At least to all appearances."

"Sure convinced me."

"That was the point, Mace. I found that it also saved me a lot of problems. You know how many girls in this town are only looking for a husband. I didn't want that. I knew I was headed out. I didn't know it was to fight fire in the Lower Forty-eight. But I knew I was leaving."

And right there, Macy considered bitterly. *That's my goddamn problem. I'm here and Tim can't wait to go again.*

"We went everywhere together, but there was no real spark. We slept together after the senior prom and the night before she left for University of Virginia or wherever it was and I went to Colorado State. I remember it was as far away as she could get. We had fun in bed, but it was more like saying goodbye and thanks than anything else for both of us."

Even though it was dark, Macy ducked her face against Tim's chest to hide her flaming cheeks. She'd always been so jealous of Sally...no, envious. She, along with every other resident of Larch Creek, had totally misread Tim Harada. He'd been with the prettiest girl in high school not for her beauty, but out of friendship. Some kind of a mutual aid society.

His hand began once more tracing over her, from butt to back, up into her hair and returning along her side.

Was that what Tim was feeling for her? Friendship?

He raised his other arm, the one her head had been pillowed on this whole time, and wrapped it around her shoulders. Against her ear she could feel his bicep ripple with easy power despite the simplicity of the gesture.

"Is that what this is? Some sort of a thank-you-for-being-a-friend fuck?" The words were out of her mouth before she'd thought about them.

Tim used his grip on her shoulders to pull her back as if now he was the one trying to see her in the dark.

TIM ALMOST WISHED it *was* just sex between friends. It would be easier that way. Have a good tumble in bed and be on their separate ways. But from the moment he'd woken with his arm around Macy Tyler's waist it hadn't been that at all.

Stroking his hand over her, he'd at first been looking for foreignness. For some strange, sick feeling of making love to your sister. Sally had told him a little of what it was like and she'd had to stop him from taking on her whole family that instant.

Instead, Macy had felt as if he'd always known she would feel that way. Every curve was a new discovery and at the same time somehow an old acquaintance.

"Well? Because if that's all this is, Harada, let me tell you exactly what you can—"

He kissed her. Tim had never found a way to stop the barrage of words that Macy could unleash once she started, so he simply kissed her.

She continued to protest for several seconds and he did as she had done on the Ladd Army Airfield; he scooped a hand deep into her hair and simply kissed her for all he was worth. When she finally let go and melted against him, it was the best feeling. This was a kiss to get lost in, to wander through and find where the sparks of heat fired up in both of them.

They didn't have to look far. There was a near-paralyzing energy between them.

His hands were still and simply held, pulling her tighter against his body, appreciating how the muscles in her behind shifted against his palm as she hooked one of those long legs over him. When had Macy grown such amazing legs?

Tim finally broke off when it simply became too much. The feeling behind the kiss was too big to fit into a friendly cuddle. It had grown until it filled the room, the house, and the forest beyond the river.

"I hope you have a license for that kiss, Harada. It should definitely not be let out in public."

"I don't even get how you can speak after that," then was surprised that he'd managed as well.

"It's a gift I have," Macy brushed a hand over his lips.

"Yeah, you never did know when to shut up, do you?"

To disprove his statement, and he knew that was the only reason she did it, she didn't say another word.

Instead, she pushed him lightly on the shoulder until he was on his back and she lay beside him with one leg hooked tantalizingly over his waist. Then just as he had earlier, she began exploring his chest with sliding fingertips that would have tickled if her touch hadn't been so sure.

Their entire first lovemaking was like that. Exploration, appreciation, and raw power. When she'd finally dug into a bedside drawer for some protection then knelt over him it had been as natural as if they'd done it a thousand times. And more powerful than when Sally had taken his virginity on prom night.

Maybe this still was Stupid Day because it felt almost as if he was losing his virginity a second time.

Sliding into Macy as she braced herself against his chest, her hair hanging down just enough to tickle his face, had centered his entire being on that single ring of soft heat slipping over him. When he was finally all the way in her, after they'd each wiggled their hips to assure they were as deeply together as they could possibly be, they stopped by unspoken mutual agreement to appreciate the sensation. Which was a good thing because the world was spinning on him and at the moment he didn't want it to stop.

And then she'd rocked her hips and it got better.

He pulled her down to lie on his chest and kissed her.

The sensations were so big that neither spoke, neither moaned, neither made a single sound. Instead, alone together in a world of perfect darkness they lost themselves in the awe-inspiring awareness of their own and each other's bodies.

Their release wasn't some huge blast of power. Tim could feel the potential for that, knew they could go there easily, so easily. Could taste how Macy's scent would change as she bucked and flailed in orgasm. But not this first time, it was too precious.

Instead it was a blooming of heat that washed over him in ocean-wave surges. The motion washed back and forth between them until the tide peaked and, leaving behind waves of even more pleasure, receded until the two of them lay spent on the sheets.

He cradled Macy against his chest. He'd been with a lot of women in his smokejumper years, but—and he tried to send an apology out with his thought—none of them had made him feel like this.

Tim felt no urge to tease, talk, check in to make sure it had been good for the woman as well. There was no need to check in with Macy, the way she held onto him told him all he needed to know.

What was surprising was the way he held onto her. It wasn't because he knew that to a woman, being held after sex was almost as important as the sex itself, maybe even more so. It wasn't because it felt so good, though it did.

Tim held onto Macy because he never wanted to let her go.

He kissed her on top of the head, and felt tears wet his chest.

"Shh," he stroked a hand over her hair and down her back. "We'll figure this out."

That was another thing he'd never said after sex, because there'd never been anything to figure out. He once again knew exactly what Macy was feeling as she continued to silently weep.

Was this what Akbar felt when he was with Laura? Gods but he hoped so for his friend's sake. It would certainly explain the changes in Akbar the Great.

Though if Tim was feeling it…

A weekend fling didn't need to be concerned about living and working in different parts of the continent. In this single act there had been no question, they hadn't been making fling, they'd been making love even this first time. That meant…

"Oh shit!" he whispered into her hair.

Macy's nod acknowledged that he'd finally caught up with why she was crying.

CHAPTER 10

overs were supposed to look different in morning's light. Weren't they?

Tim still looked...wonderful.

None of the shine had come off him as they had a midnight breakfast in a house lit only by the Alaskan mid-summer twilight.

His eyes had practically glowed with heat the moment before he'd dragged her from the table, dropped his briefs, lifted the lower edge of her long *Keep Calm, I'm a Helicopter Pilot* t-shirt, and taken her with desperate need and suddenness against the refrigerator—bottles and jars rattling together inside as she'd struggled to survive the emotions and needs doing the same within her.

They'd both collapsed back into bed after the most erotic shower of Macy's entire life. And when she awoke with his fingers stroking her, she rolled to open to his touch and ride high once more.

After she returned the favor and Tim collapsed back into a truly deep sleep, she lay there admiring him for a while.

Her lover. However briefly, there was no longer any question in her mind that he was hers or that *lover* was the operative word. This hadn't been about sex. It had been about *glorious* sex. The kind that could only occur when you cared about someone as much as they each did.

It was as if she was trying to pack in as much experience as she could as fast as she could. Like an Alaskan ground squirrel storing away pine nuts against the long winter.

Was she in love with Tim Harada?

She had been her whole life. But now he was suddenly so real, it was as if she was only just getting to know him as well.

Macy finally tore herself away and tucked the sheets up around him. She had a scheduled flight this morning to pick up some fishermen she'd dropped at a lake well in-country a week ago. They had flights back to the Lower Forty-eight this afternoon. She wouldn't think about Tim having one in a few days more. She simply wouldn't.

The blackout curtains drawn, a note on the table, and she and Baxter headed out into the shining sun of the most beautiful day she'd seen all summer.

TIM WOKE SLOWLY. And alone.

No question.

The house simply wouldn't be this quiet if Macy were around. He'd feel her vibrant energy shining like a spotlight from even the farthest corner.

He reached out to twitch one of the blackout curtains aside and let the sunlight stream into the room and received a shock. He hadn't yet seen the room in daylight and what he saw he couldn't equate with Macy Tyler, at least not the one he'd thought he knew before this trip to Alaska.

Macy had always been a slob. "A studied slob" he'd always called her, because she was so good at it that she must have practiced. Her room had always been a "no-fly zone" for Tim when they were younger. Which had made Tim honor bound to invade the inner sanctum of the disaster area as often as possible and harass her about it. Clothes, books, snow gear: all in haphazard piles on the floor. Even the posters of pop stars were crooked, overlapped, and often torn. Any furniture looked as if going through a wildfire would be an improvement.

It wasn't that the Tyler's were poor, it was that Macy was hard on everything and everyone around her.

Yet her present bedroom was neat and bright with colorful paint. There weren't any touches that he could pin down as feminine, but there was no question about the gender of the person who had designed the room. They had been sleeping and making love beneath a gorgeous quilt, clearly Ma King's work. Nobody in town had a hand like hers and this one was a gorgeous piece of local art.

Window pane, he recognized the general pattern. The whole quilt was sectioned into foot-square panes by dark strips the color of fir trees in deep summer. Each "window" was a view of Larch Creek done in multi-layered fabrics—applied, applicant, something like that. Appliqué. The river, the town, French Pete's, Denali, a group of children with a dog and a Frisbee flying so high aloft it might have been a bird. It was the story of the town he and Macy had grown up in. Even the sheets on the bed were not plain cotton, but instead a rather a rich brown flannel spangled with white snowflakes.

The walls were covered with pictures. Denali as only a pilot would see it. There were pictures of her family, including Stephen. But it wasn't a memorial, rather a celebration. Tim showed up in a number of the pictures as well, though, he was amused to notice, never once with Sally Kirkman at his side. Her hand or sneaker might be in a photo, but never the girl he'd been constantly beside in high school. Some of the pictures had obviously been cut, by there unusual narrowness.

The thing that was missing to mark it as a "girly" room was no small table with a mirror. Instead there was an old roll-top desk that could have easily dated back to French Pete himself. It was a beautiful piece and added to the richness of the room. The laptop at its center and the exercise ball rolled underneath broke the room's motif, but made it more likely that this was Macy's room.

He was oddly comforted by the absolute disaster that was going on inside the desk or he might have despaired of quite who he'd been making love to.

Tim padded out into the kitchen wearing his briefs and t-shirt. There he found the note that said Macy wouldn't be back for hours. This would be a good chance to catch up with his folks and see who was still around town. Because if Macy was here, he'd be wanting her all to himself.

He checked himself in the bathroom mirror as he used her toothbrush—after all any germs they'd owned separately last night were community property now. He didn't look like the sort of guy who would only be interested in one woman. Did he? But neither could he imagine himself in anyone else's bathroom using their toothbrush...ever again.

It was a very strange place to be in his late twenties. Maybe this was a Strange Day to make up for his Stupid Day yesterday. He now got that Macy Tyler was a woman. A woman who somehow made perfect sense in the world, flying off with her faithful dog to face the vagaries of the Alaskan wilderness and fetch outdoorsman to airports and mail bags to remote villages.

He was the one who wasn't making any sense.

Well, he'd made it through Stupid Day with life and limb intact despite jumping a fire. Then had a night of mind-altering sex. So, he'd just forge ahead and see what this day brought.

Minutes later he was still in his underwear and deciding that *strange* didn't begin to cover this day.

The jump gear and long johns that he'd spotted out on the clothesline when they'd had breakfast together were gone. Macy had probably grabbed them to return them to the BLM hangar.

His clothes were...in a locker at the Bureau of Land Management's offices at Ladd Airfield.

Nothing in Macy's closet was going to come even close.

The Harada household was on the far side of town.

Tim considered his options and discovered a variety of ways he could deeply embarrass himself, jogging across town barefoot in his underwear only one of the many unattractive options. He went for the least painful one and sighed. It still wasn't a good choice, but other than remaining a prisoner in Macy's house, he didn't see anything else he was willing to do.

Even if he did wait, the options weren't going to improve. When Macy returned the jump gear, she wouldn't know to empty out his locker. There was only one place in Larch Creek that had clothes that would fit him.

He found his phone on the kitchen counter and called his mother.

When he explained his problem, she giggled at him. Mom actually giggling.

It wasn't until after he hung up that he realized quite why.

This scene was bound to end up in her next book.

CHAPTER 11

Macy's helo still reeked of under-washed fishermen. Why did guys think that "living wild" for a week meant they had to come back stinking worse than a skunk? She'd have to ask Tim, because she sure didn't understand.

She was most of the way back to Larch Creek before she remembered Tim's smokejumper gear that she'd stashed in the LongRanger's baggage compartment to return. She had rather counted on tracking down his clothes while she was at the jumper base.

By the time she'd dithered about whether or not to circle back, she was over Liga Pass. The magnetic draw of her need for Tim made her decide to continue for home, she could dump the gear at any time... and his clothes? Well, maybe he simply wouldn't need them for a while.

She landed her LongRanger and tried not to smile at the idea of Tim trapped at her place, held prisoner by lack of any clothing that would fit.

That would only last so long. The only solution Macy could see was...

Eva Harada would simply die laughing if Macy showed up and asked for clothes for her son. This time of year there wouldn't be any convenient "dead of night" in which she could smuggle Tim sight unseen across town and into his own house. Besides, she hoped that he'd want to be with her tonight.

She wanted to head straight to Tim, instead she gritted her teeth and turned for the Harada household.

———

FRANK HARADA ANSWERED THE DOOR.

"Is it you are looking for my son?" he asked in a thick Québécois accent that she knew he only affected when he was being too pleased with himself. "Or is it perhaps his clothes you are seeking?" he shot a wicked grin at her before squatting down to greet Baxter.

Macy leaned her forehead against the doorjamb and sighed, "Either one would be a help, Mr. Harada."

"How about I lead you to both? He's here and he's not running around naked. Eva would never tolerate such a thing unless it was us doing it."

Macy's cheeks flamed hotter at the image. The tiny novelist and the tall man who managed her business, running around the house naked together. Parents weren't supposed do such things.

He waved both her and Baxter in. But after he closed the door he pulled her into a hug and held her for a long moment. It was unusual for him.

"I'm so happy for the two of you," then he kissed her on top of the head.

Oh god, now she was feeling all sniffly and that would never do.

"I'm feeling pretty happy for us as well. Confused as all get out, but I can't stop smiling."

"That's on track. A good place to begin, being happy. That is what his mother does for me, she always makes me smile." He kept an arm around her shoulders as they headed back to the kitchen.

Macy had always liked the Harada household, even when the air wasn't thick with one of Mr. Harada's amazing soups. She sniffed and guessed minestrone. Maybe "Vegetable *Barely*" as he called his meatier soups, but she didn't think so.

The ground floor made no pretentions about how a house "ought" to be. The entry from the front walk led through a mudroom, then a narrow hall with a storeroom to one side and a bathroom to the other. Then it opened into a single room that crossed the entire back of the house and took in one of the best views of the valley.

Through the large windows Denali rose majestically, commanding the eye every time. Macy had always loved coming here to watch when the winter storms ripped at the mountain. It was incredible and terrifying at the same time.

The Tyler house only had a peek-a-boo view of Denali around the edge of the McPherson's. There had been a terrible row when Mac had wanted to add an office on their side to write and print the *Lurching Larch* weekly paper. He'd finally added the office on the far side of his house but had never spoken civilly to her parents again, except when they were inside of French Pete's.

The tale went that Hilma, after chucking a pair of drunk loggers out into the snow to cool off—Hilma may have been a small woman, but no one messed with her—carved the sign over the door: *Leave your shit outside.* Ever since, French Pete's had been a haven against conflict. Except, of course, during certain sporting matches.

The Harada's great room layout was office, living room, dining, and kitchen all in a sweeping sprawl of fine woods and good taste. But it wasn't a showpiece either.

If you knew where to look, and Macy still did, the big comfortable couch had the faded stains from a blackberry ice cream fight she, Tim, and Stephen had once had. Perhaps more accurately it was a fight that she'd had when she was eight, and Tim and Stephen had survived only by intense retaliation. She could still see the spot where they'd finally managed to pin her to the couch and scrub an entire scoop of freezing cold ice cream into her hair until it might as well have been a mud pack, a frozen one.

The dining table showed the marks of a thousand school projects and she could still hear the laughter of so many meals there.

"I was just making lunch if you want to join us," Frank Harada returned to the kitchen counter.

Macy tried to speak, but couldn't as Tim stepped in the back door and stumbled to a halt of surprise and cautious wariness. At least that's what she'd expected him to do.

Instead he banged in the back door as if he were seventeen and not twenty-seven. When he spotted her, he moved straight across the room, gathered her into his arms, and kissed her. Not hard. Not with the brutal need or surprising tenderness of last night. Rather as if he simply couldn't wait to greet her.

She wanted to shove him away; she so was not ready to be kissed in this room so cluttered with childhood memories and Tim's father. And she wanted to drag him down on that couch and to hell with Frank Harada grinning to himself over hot soup and cold cut sandwiches.

Instead, when the kiss broke she managed a lame, "Hi." Deciding that it would never do to let Tim think that he so overwhelmed her senses that she couldn't function around him, she plucked at the fresh t-shirt he wore.

"So, my tactics to keep you prisoner failed. I'll have to try harder next time."

He laughed and beeped his finger on her nose just like when they were kids...and then he kissed her there.

What was a girl supposed to do with that? He wasn't upset with her for being dumb. He was amused.

She was considering how best to make him pay for that amusement—maybe there was some more blackberry ice cream in the Harada's freezer—when a ringing bell had her nearly leaping out of her skin.

"Sorry," Frank apologized.

"It's okay," Macy managed despite her pounding heart. She'd forgotten about the old tradition. When Eva Harada was writing, mealtime was announced with the clang of an old brass ship's bell that was mounted on the wall right below Eva's writing office. If she was somewhere she could stop, she'd come to the meal.

They all waited in silence for a few seconds, but there was no sound of feet moving across the upstairs office floor.

"She's in it," Frank said. "I'll make her a tray."

"No, let me." For some reason, Macy wanted to be the one to do it. When Eva had been engulfed in writing her murder mysteries, it had always fallen to one of the kids to make a meal tray and carry it up to her.

It had been most of a decade since the last time, but Macy still remembered where the cookie sheets were stowed. She spread a pretty tea towel over it. Set it with a napkin, and an unopened diet Coke with a glass of ice cubes. Frank set down a small plate with half of a roast beef sandwich and a pile of chips. Tim set a big mug of minestrone soup beside it. Macy dug a couple of chocolate chip cookies out of the jar and then bit into one of her own.

Tim leaned over and bit off the half that still stuck out of her mouth. His grin was electric and made her tingle all over as if she'd just been shocked. Tim Harada, human Taser to one Macy Tyler's nerves and emotions.

She mumbled around her half as she chewed, "You owe me a cookie, Harada."

"Half," Tim riposted.

"Whole. Interest. Besides," she swallowed and managed to clear most of her mouth, "Frank's cookies are far too good for me not to be greedy about them."

Tim's smile indicated clearly what he was feeling greedy about, and that worked for her. Later though.

She took the tray and headed up the stairs.

Macy balanced the tray on the small marble shelf that had been put there for that purpose. She knocked once lightly and swung the door open. Eva was unlikely to answer. The trick was to deliver the tray close enough so that she could easily reach for it, then sneak back out without disturbing her writing.

When she entered, Eva wasn't writing. She was sitting in the chair but facing the door.

"Even after all these years, I still recognize your light tread on the stairs. Tim and Frank could double for a cattle stampede, especially when they think they're being subtle."

"Hi, Eva. Here's your lunch."

"I'll come down and join you in a minute, but I thought we girls should have a moment together."

Macy set the tray down and tried to find somewhere to look. Just like downstairs, Denali dominated the view up here. But rather than an open welcome, Eva's office was a cozy nest lined with bookshelves that were crowded with reference books and a jumble of every genre imaginable. An eight-volume Oxford English Dictionary had a place of honor, its own shelf directly behind an oaken reading stand. There was a small desk against the back wall now covered with more books, but it had once been where Tim could do his homework.

She felt awkward pulling out his chair even if it was the only other seat in the room. Sitting in it was even more troubling. Her awareness of Tim was becoming a real problem. She could practically feel him standing directly below them and staring at the ceiling in curiosity at Macy's failure to return.

"Let him wonder," Eva said far too perceptively.

TIM WAITED another ten seconds but there were still no footsteps from either Eva or Macy returning. He looked down to see that his dad was watching him. They took their own plates and sat together at the kitchen table.

With Macy in the house Tim felt both younger and older. A part of him kept waiting for Stephen to rush up, dump his bicycle on the porch with a loud clatter, and rush in without knocking—neither the door nor the snow from his boots. And a part of him felt as if his relationship with his parents was shifting minute by minute because he and Macy had become lovers.

Tim rubbed at his forehead but couldn't make any better sense of it.

"Falling in love does that to you."

Falling in love?

His dad didn't look as if he was joking.

"Confusing the hell out of you?"

He nodded.

"Women are good at that."

Tim stared at the ceiling again.

"I—" he spoke to his dad while looking at the ceiling. Then he looked down at his dad and felt as if he was talking to the ceiling. "—don't know what to do about it. My job. My life is—" he shrugged uncomfortably. Macy was as rooted in Larch Creek as Tim was with MHA. "And hers—"

"Did I ever tell you that I was studying programming in college the year your mother came to *Université Laval* in Québec for a semester abroad?"

Tim had somehow missed that part of the story.

"I was damn good at it. Standing job offers on graduation, all of that."

"What happened?"

"This pint-sized whirlwind with Asian features, an Oklahoma accent, and a passion for language came to Laval to study French. We didn't meet until the last week before I graduated and she was due to go back to Oklahoma. I had never met anyone like her. To say we *connected* would be a complete understatement. We—"

"Too much detail," Tim raised a hand to stop him and his dad just grinned.

"Your mother said we should take the summer and drive to Alaska together. We only slept together the night before for the first time..."

Tim winced.

"...but I could never deny your mother. We left two days after graduation. We were shooting for Nome—cross the Arctic Circle and all that. We still don't know what made us turn onto this road. Wasn't any more of a road sign at the highway then than there is now. We hit Larch Creek and neither of us wanted to leave. So we didn't. It was years before we crossed the Arctic Circle even though it's only a few hundred miles north of here. She did her senior year of college at

Fairbanks. I did a lot of woodworking and other odd jobs until her writing took off. Now I'm mostly her assistant which makes a surprising amount of use of my computer skills. I do a nice side business doing the indie publishing work for most of the writers in town."

Tim had known the end of the story, but not the beginning.

"What are you saying? Mace and I should run away to Oklahoma or something?"

"Could do worse things."

Tim had been to Oklahoma to visit Grandpop. Flat. No dense forests. The only kind of wildfires were grassland burns, most quickly beaten. Certainly no smokejumpers. Definitely not.

Again he looked at the ceiling.

Options. They had been lovers a single night and already he was worried about what would happen when they talked options.

He'd never tried to do that with a woman before.

Even in his professional life there'd never been any real discussions. It had been Akbar who had led the way from Colorado to California to MHA in Oregon. Tim had just been glad to fight fires beside his friend.

He had a sneaking suspicion that the answers weren't going to be so obvious this time.

"IT'S TOO SOON, EVA," Macy blurted it out and then wished she could take it back. "We only just—" she managed to stop that one before it came out. She wished she wasn't sitting in Tim's childhood chair in Eva's office. It made her body far too aware of what they had "only just."

"But you've loved him since you were a teenager," Eva didn't make it a question.

"Since I can remember," she nodded miserably.

"He has the same problem, sweetheart. You just need to give him a little time to figure it out."

"He *what?*" that got her attention back to Eva's face.

"Did he ever show you any of his writing?" Macy tried to make sense of Eva's subject change, but couldn't.

"I didn't know Tim could spell his way out of *Winnie the Pooh.*" Tim had always been a good student at school, but she'd never heard about any writing.

Eva pointed a slim finger over Macy's head.

She turned to look at the shelf above the small desk. There were a half-dozen manuscripts stacked there.

"Tim's," Eva confirmed before she could ask the question. "He's good, some real potential there. Young work, naïve, but solid. Wrote those in high school. He loved writing, but ran out of time to focus."

"What's your point?" How did she not know that about Tim? She thought she knew everything there was to…but she hadn't known about the truth behind his relationship with Sally Kirkman either. Since when had the boy she knew better than anyone on the planet become an inscrutable man?

Macy studied the shelf a moment longer. From watching Mom's labors over her science fiction manuscripts, Macy knew enough to judge that there was an immense amount of work sitting there. That much work couldn't be done without passion.

Eva hopped to her feet and gathered up her lunch tray. Macy rose, opened the office door, and held it for her.

"My point is," Eva stopped close beside Macy and looked up at her, "he thought he was writing action adventure, but he really wrote romances. Good powerful love stories lie at the core of every one of those stories."

"And?" Mr. Macho Smokejumper writing romances was actually a pretty funny image that she rather liked about him. But Macy still wasn't seeing it.

Eva moved out into the hall, "As I said, he wrote them in high school. I'm positive that he wouldn't realize it, but as an only some-what biased reader, I did notice that his heroines always looked much alike."

"Sally Kirkman."

Eva shook her head, then her grin went wicked. "None of them looked like dear Sally."

Macy felt numb enough to stupidly ask the next question. "Then who?" There was little question that she didn't actually want to know the answer.

"It's a common enough mistake for a young writer, to make all of their heroes or heroines look alike. Especially when they're in love," Eva then nodded along the upstairs hall before carrying her tray down the stairs.

Macy tried to follow, honestly she did.

But her feet were frozen to the floorboards. She couldn't look away from where Eva had indicated at the end of the hall.

Macy stared at the reflection in the big mirror that hung there.

Her own reflection.

CHAPTER 12

"*You never told me* about your writing."

Tim grunted. It was all he could manage. How was it that women were able to talk the moment after amazing sex? All his body wanted to do was melt into Macy's mattress and never move again.

"Why?"

He shrugged and enjoyed the way her head rode on his shoulder where she'd curled up against him, once he'd managed to roll his weight off her.

"Give, Harada."

Please, just a moment to relax into the warm moment.

She slipped a hand down his chest, past his waist, and clamped onto him.

"Okay, Tyler! Okay."

Then Baxter decided that the fact they were talking was an excuse to jump on the bed and place a clawed foot in Tim's gut before circling and flopping down to lie against his other side.

"Geez, a guy just can't get a break around here."

"Nope," Macy sounded entirely too cheery.

Tim thought back. He forgotten about the writing. Between wildfires and willing women, he'd found plenty of other things to keep him busy in more recent years.

"I think I started because it gave me an excuse to be with Mom. I knew I couldn't disturb her when she was writing. No matter how patient she thinks she is, I learned early to read the deep frustration each time one of my questions ripped her out of a story. Though she was always cool about it."

Macy snuggled in closer, still holding him, but thankfully gently now. Baxter sighed happily against his other side. Tim kept one arm around Macy's shoulders, but scratched Baxter with his other hand. There was a surprising rightness to the moment, as if he somehow belonged right here.

"So, I started writing. There was this one short story for English class that I'd been rather proud of. Mom read it and said it was a good idea for a novel. So I just started writing it. It became a thing we did on quiet summer mornings when the sun wakes you up way too early. Kind of became a thing we shared over the years. We just wrote together."

She paused and he could see a question skirting across the edges of her thoughts. Edges? More like a neon sign flashing above her head. Then he felt the tension slip out of her body as she set it aside for now and asked something else.

"Writing became a *thing?*"

"Uh-huh." It was obvious that Macy was about to pith him with something, but he couldn't imagine what.

"You're not very erudite after sex, are you?" she began nuzzling his neck and massaging him with the gentle hand still slipped down between his legs.

"Sure. I can be. No problem." He couldn't even build a decent sentence at the moment. "At least I could after sex with any other woman. Where did you learn that last thing, anyway? No. I don't want to know, but it was amazing."

"Uh," Macy's hand stilled and she rolled her face into his shoulder for a moment. "I'm a big fan of Dorothy's urban fantasy," she mumbled into his chest.

Tim tried not to picture that, but it was difficult once the image was planted in his brain. Dorothy Quinn might be a recluse and old enough to be his grandmother, but her books were undeniably hot. Copies hidden deep in knapsacks had been all the rage in high school, probably still were.

"I," Tim had to clear his throat. He could feel himself start to laugh.

Macy's giggle into his shoulder was both charming and contagious.

He did his best to resist joining in. "I must have missed that one," he managed to say with a suitably dry tone.

Rather than collapsing into a fit of merry giggles, she lifted her head off his shoulder and studied his face for a moment.

"What?"

"Well then there's something else you don't know about." Macy shooed Baxter back off the bed and proceeded to show him.

Neither of them felt inclined to giggle for long.

Macy didn't kill him with kindness, but she came darn close.

CHAPTER 13

*T*im had *Natalie on* the run, at least he hoped he did.

They sat at the bar in French Pete's and who paid for the plate of onion rings they were both eating was on the line; Tim or Carl. Carl wasn't looking very worried about it, with good reason Tim had to admit. Losing a game of chess to a ten-year old, well, he wished Akbar was here so that she could be trouncing his behind instead.

Funny, he hadn't thought about Akbar much since early in the Arctic Village Fire. He'd initially kept asking himself, "How would Akbar approach this? What line of attack would he use? How to balance the resources against time to best—" Finally, he'd run out of time for even that simple a luxury. He'd reacted as his training had told him to.

Oregon felt a million miles away at the moment. French Pete's, on the other hand, was humming this morning. The quilters were at the big corner table today. Ma King, a big, round Native woman with astonishingly delicate needlework, had the seat of honor close to the front window where the light was best.

Dorothy Quinn came in and set her quilting bag beside Ma. He knew there was some overlap between the writers and the quilters, but why today of all days?

She spotted him and crossed to the bar to greet him.

"Timmy! How are you, boy?" She made *boy* sound like he was a street punk about the get his behind whipped and she'd be the woman to do it. She was a tough old bird.

He attempted to speak, but he'd have better luck speaking to Macy *while* they were having sex, which was completely the wrong thought at the moment.

So, he blushed and Dorothy cackled with that evil-witch laugh of hers that had always creeped him out as a kid. She didn't even have the decency to need a moment before she understood that there was no way he could speak to the author of what Macy had just done to him.

She was humming merrily to herself as she strutted back to sit beside Ma King.

When Natalie asked what that was all about, he refused to answer, even if it took his cheeks a long time to return to normal color.

Oregon was *definitely* a million miles away. A million miles and just three more days.

But he couldn't think about that. He attacked Natalie's bishop and immediately lost a pawn and his own bishop on the next turn in exchange for his troubles.

He would allow himself two more days to focus on only the here and now. It was something Tim was usually pretty good at, just living in the moment.

Wildland firefighting was like that. On the fire, other than brief planning sessions, there was only the moment. The pain, exhaustion, and heat combined into an endless blur of events mostly indistinguishable; except at one end was a raging inferno and at the other a brutal terrain covered by wide smoldering stretches of the Black.

Off the fire was oddly similar, without the pain, heat, and exhaustion. You prepped, you trained, and you played. But it mostly blurred together until the moment the fire call came and interrupted all other pursuits.

The problem with this moment was how much he was enjoying it.

"Checkmate," Natalie announced.

Okay, most of it.

"At least you played a little better than Macy. She was really off her game."

Which made Tim feel a little better, but not much. The problem was that this was about as well as he ever played. Chess wasn't one of his strengths.

"This kid wipe you out?" Macy's dad came up to look over the final layout of the chessboard.

"She did me out of a half plate of onion rings," Tim dropped a couple of dollars on the bar beside the empty plate.

"Way to go, champ," Josh Tyler congratulated Natalie. "Are you planning to grow up to be a chess hustler?"

"I've considered it. Thank you for the game and the onion rings, Mr. Harada," then she picked up her book—with a cover that didn't look as hot as one of Dorothy's but otherwise not much less gruesome —and Tim felt suddenly invisible.

Macy's dad pointed to one of the tables, "Keep me company for lunch. Lisa is over with the gang."

Macy's mom waved when he looked over. She was an older, less chaotic version of her daughter. Macy's brash turned to elegance.

"Glad to, Mr. Tyler." Though now that he was sleeping with Macy, maybe not so much.

Eight or nine women were now gathered around the table with Ma King. He'd been a couple years behind Ma King's daughter who was now one of the group. There was one other girl of the same age, who he didn't recognize, but most of them were at least empty-nester age or older. Dorothy said something. The whole group turned to look at him, including Lisa Tyler, then there was a huge burst of laughter.

Tim chose the seat with his back to them. Maybe being defeated by Natalie was going to be the least painful part of this day.

"At some point I have to cease being 'Mr. Tyler.' That worked when I was your teacher twenty years ago, but I'm retired now, so you may cease and desist."

"I don't know, Mr. Tyler—"

"I understand that old habits die hard, but third grade was a long time ago and—"

"It's not that at all. It's that Natalie seems to suddenly think I'm Mr. Harada. When did I become that?"

Josh Tyler rubbed his chin, but Tim suspected that he was trying to hide a smile.

"And when did you retire?" the words had finally registered along with the surprise. Part of the order of the universe was the progression of the K-6 teachers at Larch Creek, one per year.

"Last year. It frees me up to travel with Lisa when she goes to conventions or a movie set. In between, I take up the occasional tourist. Remember that old plane that I was always fixing up?"

"Are you kidding me?" The old Stearman B-75 had made Mr. Tyler beyond cool as a teacher. When he was finally able to fly it, the whole town had come out to watch the first flight.

"She's all pretty now. I painted her bright red—"

"Just like in that movie, *The Kid.*" Tim felt like he was about twelve with excitement.

"Exactly," Mr. Tyler looked terribly pleased.

They were about to order when Carl's ham radio crackled to life behind the bar. Everyone in the restaurant shushed to listen. Natalie even looked up from her book.

"Carl, you there?" Despite the poor reception, Tim didn't need her call sign to recognize Macy's voice.

Carl picked up the mic, "Go ahead, Macy."

"Is Dad around?" He was already out of his chair and headed to the bar. Tim followed him over.

"Here, honey? What's up?"

"I had a part failure after dropping off that hunting party. I landed safely, but I can't jury-rig a fix. Can you fetch a part for me at Fairbanks and drop it down to me?"

"Sure," he scribbled down notes of what she needed and where she had landed. It was an awkward spot a half dozen miles west of Larch Creek. It was out in one of the numerous dead zones of Alaska where there were neither roads nor villages.

When he finished, he turned to Tim, "Want to go for a ride?"

"Heck, yeah."

Mr. Tyler laughed, "Macy said that you never swear, not even when…" He trailed off leaving no doubt of the topic of his conversation with his daughter.

"During sex?" Natalie asked from close beside his elbow.

Tim did his best not to groan; this wasn't happening. Please, this wasn't happening.

Carl handed them a bag with a couple of sandwiches as they headed for the door, "I'll make fresh for the ladies." He nodded to the quilters.

They had to pass dangerously close to the big table to reach the front door.

A whole series of well meant and wholly embarrassing titters followed him out the door.

"She's beautiful, Mr. Tyler." And she was. The Stearman biplane wasn't just red, it was lipstick red and shined to a such a gloss that Tim could easily see himself in the finish. Though she was only twenty-five feet long, thirty across the wings, and ten high, she looked like a street fighter or a boxer, tough and ready. Her tail rested on the ground which made her big nine-cylinder radial engine look ready to punch a hole skyward even sitting still. The seven-foot wooden prop had been burnished until it shone.

"Thanks, and if you don't call me Josh, you don't get to fly in her."

"Yes, sir, Mr. Josh, sir."

"Sass," he sounded disgusted but the smile was genuine. "You *have* been sleeping with my daughter."

Not *sleeping* so much…Tim kept that thought to himself.

The slap on his back told him that he hadn't succeeded at even doing that. Wait! He'd never mentioned that they were—

"No secrets in a small town, Tim. Besides, I've never seen her smile so much."

Tim bit his tongue hard to keep still. There was no way to win today.

They rolled it out of the southern hangar. Macy's helo had been parked in the northern one. There were a number of other planes tucked into either hangar, most in varying states of decay or restoration, but only a couple were flight-worthy. If any of the others were finally fixed up, Larch Creek would have to add a third hangar along the highway.

It was only a matter of minutes before they were aloft and soaring upward toward Liga Pass. The valley lay open below. Heinrich's barley fields made smooth-looking surfaces of a uniform summer-green that rippled in long waves. Maxine's land was a kaleidoscope of bright chard, dark beet, pale lettuce, onion, carrot, and a dozen other crops at a few acres each. Heinrich supplied the best makings for barley beer and Maxine kept an entire valley of canners supplied with everything they'd need for the long winter.

"They still fight?" Tim asked over the intercom.

"Cats and dogs," Josh told. "Have been ever since Heinrich was forced to sell her half his land."

"Forced?"

"Long story. There's a reason Carol is the way she is. With those two as parents, how could she not be."

"Uh, yeah. I suppose." Tim hadn't known that Carol was their daughter, which made Natalie their granddaughter. It was hard to imagine. Of course, it was far harder to imagine Heinrich and Maxine had ever been married. How had he missed this whole saga? By being young, self-absorbed, and preoccupied with sports and girls.

Descending over the back side of the pass, Josh did a side roll, wing over wing, a long, lazy move that had Tim hanging on for dear life. Which had made him let go of Carl's lunch bag. As Tim watched it tumble out and fall toward the trees below, he hoped that whatever wolf or bear found it liked horseradish on his roast beef sandwiches.

"Been working on my aerobatic rating," Josh told him over the radio that connected them. "I wasn't supposed to do that yet without an instructor aboard and don't worry, you aren't getting a loop. Come back next year and I'll give you a heck of a ride."

"Remind me not to do that." Tim was in the forward open cockpit. Josh had provided him with all the right gear even including a leather helmet, goggles, and a white scarf. "Bet this is a big hit with the tourists."

"They do love it. Macy and I try to schedule the mountain flybys at the same time so that we can take photos of each other. Those sell really well."

They were down at Fairbanks Airfield in under fifteen minutes from take-off. What would be an hour's car drive over the winding pass and down the highway to Fairbanks zipped by quickly at a hundred and fifty miles an hour.

Josh had called ahead and someone ran a part out to them on the flight line. By request, it was already rolled up in bubble wrap in a bright red plastic baggie. They could fly over, drop it out from a hundred feet up, and she'd have the part in minutes.

Tim was relegated with the job of dropping the part. He tucked it tight between his knees just in case Josh had another roll waiting for him.

Macy had gone down on the other side of Larch Creek from Fairbanks, so it took just as long to double back and reach her. Tim didn't mind, the shining blue sky and solid roar of the massive engine made it easier not to talk. Or even think. He simply sat back and enjoyed the ride, though the sandwich would have been good right about now.

Was that what he and Macy were doing? Simply enjoying the ride while it lasted? He couldn't think of when he'd had such fun being with a woman, probably never. The problem was that he didn't want it to end. Maybe his idea of just cruising for two days and then facing reality together on the last day wasn't as good as it had sounded a few hours ago.

Tonight maybe. They'd get out, be with other people a little. Maybe he'd take her to dinner. A nice dinner.

"Hey Josh. Is Aviators still the best steakhouse in town?"

"Thinking of taking my little girl out for some courting?"

Tim wished it was that simple. "I think it's time we had a talk."

Josh's reply was a low whistle of sympathy and he replied in a serious tone. "I find I'm rather torn. I'm thrilled you two feel that way about each other. And I'm afraid that's going to be a talk with some tough questions for both of you. Yes, Aviators is still the best. It's a good choice, get out of town so you can both think."

Tim stared back out at the landscape. They were in rough forest now. The north flanks of the Alaska Range tore up the land here into hard country. Sharp hills and ridges, deep river and glacier-cut valleys. The forests that climbed over them had a surprising number of brown and dead trees.

"Sawflys," Josh told him. "Bad problem with the warming climate. They're damaging and killing huge numbers of trees. Gets any warmer and we'll have the spruce beetle moving inland. It has already started killing trees along the coast."

What Tim saw when he looked down was tinder. A lot of tinder. If this area lit off it wasn't going to be some comfortable burn that could be allowed to run its course to clear the forest floor of deadfall and renew the soils. It was going to be a bad fire that would slash a hundred thousand acres out of the landscape faster than you could blink.

"There she is," Josh called out.

Josh didn't know to call out "ten o'clock low." Tim had to twist around to see where he was looking. Figures, Tim was looking over the wrong side of the plane.

He stared down as they roared by. It was the first time he felt any fear for Macy. Her helicopter was parked at the bottom of a deep valley. Her skids were in a stream and trees were crowded close to either side. He couldn't imagine how she'd land there when everything was operational, never mind when there was something broken.

So much at risk due to a part he could hold between his knees?

He was having trouble breathing. Real trouble. Bad enough that it could almost be a pile of shattered helicopter below, not merely a broken one.

Macy waved as the red biplane roared over and then rocked its wings side to side as it flew into sight over the valley wall.

She grabbed her radio, "Hi Daddy."

"Hey, Baby. We'll get you on the next pass."

We? Oh. No need to ask. Of course Tim would be up there. Having a long talk with her father about...Macy sighed. She didn't want to do a thing that might harm the few precious days they had left, but she was enough of a realist to know that the time for them to talk was sooner, not later. She hated being a realist.

The need to talk, now acknowledged, made her rather ticked off that he was up there and she was down here. If the time was soon, now was as good a soon as any.

The heavy roar started in the south end of the valley. She could hear the engine, feel its deep bass notes, before it came into sight around a curl in the little valley where she'd landed. He was so low that it nearly made her heart stop, but he was the one up there, so he must have a good, clear view.

She could see the front passenger lean out to the side, a bright red package clutched in both hands. With near perfect timing, he let it go.

Of course it was near perfect. Smokejumpers probably knew more than anyone about delivering items from the air.

It splashed into the stream not a hundred feet south of her Long-Ranger and washed right down to her. She didn't even have to step into the ice-cold flow, just balanced on two rocks and plucked it out of the water.

"Hole in one!" she radioed up. She unwrapped it quickly. Exactly the throttle linkage she needed. "You done good. I already started ripping out the old parts, so I should have this fixed up in about an hour. See you for dinner, sweetheart."

There was a several beat delay.

Then it was her father's laughter that came back over the airwaves. "You got him with that one, Macy. He's speechless. So I'll—"

"No I'm not. Surprised is all. Just be careful, Mace. I love you."

Macy was glad her radio was clipped to her belt or she'd have dropped it in the water.

"Uh," Tim still had the transmit key down, so she could only listen. Unlike telephones, radios were one-way devices. "Did I really just say that? Holy shit!"

"Release the mic key, Tim, or we'll never know what she's going to say back," her father told him. With a sharp click the radio frequency was available again.

What in the world was she supposed to say to that? How could he drop the L-bomb on her over an open radio frequency?

She could imagine the waiting silence in the plane circling above. And the sudden silence in French Pete's as everyone turned to stare at Carl's radio *always on* behind the bar. Half the town would know by now that she'd gone down and would be listening to make sure the part was delivered. Larch Creek was a small town and her going down alone in the wilderness would make big enough news as it was. She was definitely a front page item of next week's *Lurching Larch*.

By now she had an audience that probably counted upward of a hundred people, all of whom knew her and her family. Including the people who *were* her family like her father flying above her right now.

How the hell was she supposed to respond under those circumstances?

"Tim?" she clicked off.

He responded with a careful, "Yes?"

"Telling me that you love me, is that what it takes to finally make you swear?"

Again an overlong pause, "Appears so." But she could feel his careful smile as he looked down on her.

"Oh," she did her best to sound normally cheery, "I've always wondered what it would take. I'll let you know when I'm airborne. Tyler out."

The silence from above was deafening.

Her father finally came back with, "Roger. Tyler the elder returning to base. Over and out." She gave him points for managing not to laugh in poor Tim's ear. He waggled his wings and was gone.

Macy had to sit down on a rock for a moment.

Tim loved her.

She'd never said those words to anyone since Stephen had died. "The words died with my brother," she'd apologized to Billy back when she'd thought he was still marriage-worthy.

Macy hadn't said those words to Tim, but she was surprised to realize she could have.

And she would, soon.

But before she tried, she first had to fix her helo and then get Tim somewhere half the town wasn't listening.

CHAPTER 14

"Well, that was news."

Tim stared straight ahead and ignored Josh Tyler's teasing tone from the seat behind him. The only other woman he'd ever said that to had given birth to him. He and Sally had talked about it, but only to determine that they weren't in love.

But for Macy, the words had slipped out on their own and—

"What's that?"

"What's what?" Josh had been turning the biplane for home causing Tim's gaze to sweep across the rolling landscape with the turn.

"There!" he pointed west. "Turn back."

Josh altered the bank of the plane. "I don't see anything."

Tim blinked a couple of times and then swung his head side to side to make sure that what he was seeing wasn't light reflecting on a smear on his goggles. It wasn't.

"Keep going. Get me down lower."

"Where are we going, Tim?"

"There, see that bit of white down in the trees?" They continued in silence for several seconds. The biplane had been flying just above stall speed—the slowest it could safely go—to make the part-drop more accurate. Two miles west of where Macy had gone down, there was a little puff of white.

"Just a small cloud," Josh insisted. "You see them all the time as if they were caught in the tree branches. Or maybe a campfire of those hunters she dropped off."

The next puff wasn't white, it was gray-brown.

"Get us over it, as low as you can." Tim had seen those signs before. When a lightning storm had passed through the night before, but started no fires. Or at least appeared not to. But some superheated tree trunk or rotting groundcover could catch a whiff of oxygen hours or even days later. Then it didn't just bloom into fire, it often exploded.

The next puff had some black in it.

"Keep the smoke to the side. Don't pass directly into it."

"Roger that," Josh sounded serious now. He swung alongside it and banked into a turn so they could look sideways out of the plane and try to spot the origin as it circled.

"Give me the BLM fire frequency."

"You're on."

"Hank, this is Tim. You there?"

"Hi, lover boy. You do know that we monitor the general aviation frequency, don't you?"

He did now. And that meant that he'd told Macy he loved her all the way out to Ladd Airfield and…oh man she was going to be ticked about that one. He decided that no comment was the best answer.

"You've got a burn."

Josh read the coordinates off his GPS.

"Starting small but hot like a lightning strike," Tim reported.

"There hasn't been a cloud in the sky for weeks."

Tim stared down as the biplane continued to circle. He could see the fire spreading rapidly through the undergrowth. It was already fifty feet across and growing.

On the next circle he spotted a clearing upwind to the west. A clearing big enough to land a helicopter and drop off a team of hunters. Fire origin was the Fire Marshall's job, but there wasn't a smokie on the planet who wouldn't point right to the hunters.

"While we've been talking it has jumped from a dozen feet to an acre and—Bank left, Josh. Do it now!"

As the Stearman biplane twisted away from the fire, a burst of flame roared aloft. Not up to their height, but that wasn't something he wanted to be flying near.

"Hank, we now have a crown fire." It was no longer only the undergrowth that was on fire. The fire had climbed high into the thick trees where it could jump from treetop to treetop driven by the wind. "Call your team. We just flashed over into two acres."

"Roger that. We're thirty minutes out."

No need to acknowledge that either way. Thirty minutes to this fire could easily mean thirty more acres.

"Are we okay to head back?" Josh took them back aloft.

"I suppose," Tim ached to get down to the fire, but there was no way and he didn't have his gear or a team. "Nothing else we can do from up here."

Then, moments later, they flew over the valley where Macy's helicopter lay.

She'd said an hour to fix it.

Tim twisted in his seat to stare at the fire beyond the tail of the plane. It was too early for it to develop much of a smoke plume, but he'd been right. This dried-out landscape was going to make for a very angry and fast-moving fire. The steady westerly wind was going to work like a bellows on the flames.

Josh also twisted in his seat to look behind them and then back down at his daughter before turning to Tim. His wide eyes behind the goggles said that Josh could see the bad news, too.

Tim tapped his earpiece and Josh nodded as soon as he had the radio reset to the general aviation frequency.

"Hi Mace. Tim here. How is that repair going?" He kept his tone light. No point in scaring civilians, even when they were civilians as competent as Macy Tyler.

"Faster if you weren't interrupting me." Her voice was a laugh and a caress.

"You always were too cute for your own good."

"I'm not cute, I'm beautiful. I know because you told me."

"You're both," he wasn't about to argue. "How long?"

"Slow. I'm guessing closer to two hours. Be easier if there was more than one of me. Now leave me alone. I have work to do."

They flew in silence for a long moment before Josh asked him over the intercom, "Does she have two hours?"

Tim shook his head and tried not to pound the dash in frustration. "Where's the nearest parachute? At the hangar? That's over twenty minutes round trip. Or Fairbanks…" which was closer to an hour and made him feel positively ill.

"Nope," Josh sounded oddly pleased.

"Where then?" He'd always known that nobody in the Tyler household could answer a straight question with a straight answer.

"When I rebuilt the Stearman, I wanted her to be as authentic as possible, but I didn't want to scare the passengers."

"And…" Tim ground his teeth.

"Pilots would wear parachutes when they flew these kites. Me? I stowed them under the seats. You're sitting on one."

Tim reached down and wrapped his fingers around a thick, plastic-wrapped package. He pulled it out and recognized the brand as one of the top ram-air chutes available.

"If you were a woman, Josh, I'd marry you right now!" Tim scrabbled open the package and began wrestling his way into the harness.

"If you marry my daughter, I expect we'll both call it good."

Tim froze with the harness buckled around one leg and the opposite shoulder.

"If I—" was all he managed because his lungs had stopped working as well.

Suddenly there was no air flow to his voice or oxygen to his brain. He felt as if he was floating and the Stearman was in a long, weightless dive that would leave him crashed upon the earth.

"If I—" he tried again with just as little success.

"Oops! Sorry." Josh Tyler didn't sound the least bit sorry.

Tim resumed his struggle to get into the harness in a confined space. Once he managed it, he turned again to glare at Josh in the cockpit behind him.

Josh handed him a portable radio.

"Now go down there and get the girl we both love home safe."

Tim nodded and double-checked his gear.

"Hank packed the chutes for me."

"He's good. Take me in at two thousand feet up and along the ridgeline to the west above Mace." When Josh nodded, Tim pulled off his headset to the plane's intercom. The roar of the radial engine became gigantic and the wind an equally solid roar.

He eyed the smoke plume. It had reached a few thousand feet but still wouldn't be visible from down in Macy's valley, yet. His early assessment had been right. This terrain was going to burn fast and hot.

Tim clambered out of the cockpit and stepped onto the wing, staying crouched so that he didn't bang his head on the upper wing. He moved to the trailing edge of the wing and held onto the edge of Josh's cockpit.

"Never thought I'd have a wing walker," Josh shouted at him. "Makes me feel like the old barnstorming days. That would have been fun." The man had an innate cheerfulness, one of the many gifts he'd passed on to his children.

Then he rested a hand on Tim's, "You've come long way since third grade. You're a good man."

The gesture. The kindness from a man who'd lost his son and was now trusting his daughter's safety into Tim's hands had him shifting his weight from foot to foot in his low squat.

Josh glanced ahead, then raised his hand to flash: five, four...

"Thanks, Mister Tyler," he did his best to make it sound like third-grader awe.

A glance over his shoulder and he could spot the ridge and Macy's helo.

Josh's countdown timing was close.

Tim faced the stern, made sure he knew where the Stearman's empennage was so that he didn't jump into a piece of the tail, and reminded himself that he had to pull his own ripcord—no static lines on a Stearman.

Josh flashed one and then a fist.

Tim waited an extra second for the best timing and then tumbled off the wing in a tuck-roll that would guarantee he lost enough altitude before the tail caught up with him. The roar of the plane was gone and he enjoyed a moment flying free in the streaming wind. Then he popped the chute and circled down toward Macy.

She stopped work to stare up at him with a fist on one hip and the other hand shading her eyes.

He took one last look at the smoke plume, which hadn't changed in the previous ten seconds, and then it disappeared from sight as he descended into the valley.

The steady westerly wind had pushed him out over the center of the valley as he'd planned. But down in the gut of it, the breezes were a little chaotic. Nothing like when jumping a fire, so he managed to land neatly close beside the broken LongRanger.

Macy picked her way over the rocks as he gathered and stuffed the chute back in the bag.

"That eager to see me, huh?"

Tim was a little surprised at just how true that was. Macy painted a picture in her boots, jeans, and tight t-shirt that proclaimed: *Helicopter Pilot, because Badass isn't an official job title.* Her hair caught in the wind and her smile caught in the sunlight. A smudge of grease on her right cheek and a Bell LongRanger helicopter parked in the wilderness for a backdrop. She belonged here. Right here. She took his breath away.

"That eager to see you? Nah. Just figured you'd be lost without a guy's help."

She snorted out a laugh and he kissed her.

Time was precious, a fire was coming, but some things took priority. He was kissing the woman he loved and she was kissing him back in a way that left no doubt to her answer. Things changed after you said you loved someone.

Their kisses had ranged from initially tentative to brain-numbing, body-jolting erotic. But now Tim noticed everything, the way she sighed as she moved against him, the way her hair smelled of the Alaskan outdoors and the way his hands felt where they wrapped around her waist, as if they'd been formed to hold this specific woman.

"If we can find a soft patch of grass, this repair may take three hours," she murmured when he finally released her.

That snapped him back to reality, "We have less than one."

"We what?" her voice was still hazy from the kiss as his would be if he hadn't seen what was going on over the ridge.

As if in answer, the radio on his hip crackled to life, "Tim, this is Hank. We're airborne in ten. One of the SEATs is down for maintenance. I've put out a call for Macy Tyler for backup, but haven't been able to reach her yet. I left a voice mail."

Macy squinted up at Tim in alarm.

"Roger, Hank. I've got her here, outside of cell service. She's had a mechanical failure; we're trying to get her airborne. You'll see us when you arrive, we're in the valley due east of the blaze. Set up on the ridgeline immediately to the west of Macy's position; it's going to be our first hold point and it'll be a scramble to make it work. As soon as we have Macy's helo repaired, I'll send her for her bucket."

Macy mouthed, "A fire?" while he was talking to Hank.

He nodded, pointed west, swung his arm to show it growing.

"Your smokejumper gear is still in the back of my helo," she whispered. "I forgot to return it the other day."

He squeezed her shoulder in thanks and continued talking to Hank, "Also, I have basic gear, but I could use a full harness and a shelter. Oh, and a Pulaski fire axe."

"Full kit. Got it. Out," and Hank was gone.

"We need you aloft, Mace, so lets get some hustle on."

"You seemed to have a lot of time to spare for that kiss," she complained as they hurried back over the rocks toward the LongRanger.

"I thought you'd be happy that I had my priorities straight," he followed after her. This time it didn't bother him in the slightest as he appreciated the tight jeans she wore.

"Best kiss of my life. A wildfire on its way to kill my helicopter. Hmm," Macy made a considering hum as they reached the broken helo, but she didn't sound too displeased with his choice.

MACY APPRECIATED TIM'S HELP. The broken part was inside the top of the helicopter, close beside the main rotor assembly. She'd have had to run down to the ground a dozen different times for a tool or waste time scrounging through her spares pouch for a washer or some other small part. With Tim's help she was able to sit here and work; and try not to think about the fire crawling toward them.

One nice thing about Tim was that he listened to her—something Billy had never done. And let her take the lead, which he'd also done any number of times while they'd been making love—yet another black mark against Billy.

She finally managed to pop free the last bushing on the broken linkage, it had been badly bent when it failed and she'd been trying desperately to get a control response as she'd autorotated down into the steep-walled valley.

Macy wondered what she'd seen in Billy to begin with. About all he had going for him was that he was tall...

"Oh shit!"

"What?" Tim rushed up to her from where he'd been digging the smokejumper gear out of the rear baggage compartment.

"I just figured out why I almost married Billy Wilkins."

"You did what?" Tim's shock sounded deep and profound.

"Your mom never told you?" No. Obviously not. Her son was gone from Alaska; what would be the point. "He was a...I don't know. An aberration in judgment." And she wasn't going to mention, that he'd been almost the exact height and build of Tim Harada. The only things the two men had in common.

"You almost married someone?"

"Maybe I should warn you, I broke his nose and busted out a couple of teeth on the altar."

"I'm forewarned. Any particular reason?"

Macy held the new part in place and considered the best order to install it. This end first, "Could you hand me the tube of grease from the toolkit and a pair of needle-nose pliers."

Tim dug them out and reached up to her perch atop the Long-Ranger to slap them into her hand surgeon style.

"How do you feel about three ways?" she made her voice Billy Wilkins' low and stupid, but of course Tim being Tim took the question at face value.

"Three-way whats?"

If Macy wasn't greasy and racing a wildfire to save her helo, she'd go down and kiss him right now.

"Oh, you mean like…" he trailed off and eyed her carefully.

She kept her attention on the repair and waited to see where he went with it.

"I guess… I mean… I was always a fan of the one man-one woman idea. If I'm with someone, it's them I want to be paying attention to… Not…"

Macy considered going down and doing more than just kissing him, but there simply wasn't time.

"I…" he tried once more to speak in a fit of caution.

She finally decided to let him off the hook, "Good. Because if you love me, I want it to be *me* that you love. I'm selfish that way."

"I do love you," Tim insisted without a hint of caution in his voice. He handed her the cotter pin to anchor the part in place. Then he must have connected the pieces of her question and burst out laughing. "Which explains the bloody nose on the altar."

"Broken nose. And missing teeth," Macy corrected him and slid in the cotter pin and bent it with the needle-nose pliers. "And I love you."

That stopped her repair job. She had to sit there for a moment and make sure she could still breathe. Getting dizzy and falling off the top of her helicopter would hurt on these rocks.

"Wow!" she remarked when she was sure she was still conscious and functioning. "I see why you swore, Tim. Those words slip out so easily when they're true."

"I noticed that myself."

They traded smiles. He brushed a hand over her foot where it dangled down the side of the helicopter, and then began stripping off his clothes.

Macy allowed herself the time to watch him peel down to his underwear. Mostly naked in the wilderness, Tim Harada was a revelation. Whack her on the head with a club and drag her into the nearest cave. His body wasn't merely a beautiful example of male fitness, it drew her right down to the very core.

She was definitely going to have to bring him out into the wilderness…when there wasn't a wildfire thinking about cooking them for lunch. Macy went back to work, but couldn't help glancing over at Tim as he transformed once more before her eyes—this time into serious dude in his Nomex armor ready to face the flaming beast.

———

"GOT YOU IN SIGHT, BUDDY," Hank called down as the Sherpa C-23 jump plane buzzed by over the valley.

"Still look like the ridge is the place?" Tim handed up some more tools to Macy, willing her fingers to move faster—not that they probably could have. The girl…the woman was putting on some serious hustle; competence rolled off her in waves.

"Ridge is definitely our best shot, but you weren't kidding about we need to hurry. We're jumping now. You better get Macy's bird out of there and fast."

"Can't rush perfection," Macy called down to him from where she was still working.

He didn't pass on the comment.

Tim eyed the valley wall. He didn't want to leave Macy's side until she was airborne, but it was going to take a good half hour to climb out of here and get up to the fight.

"Do me a favor, Tim?"

"Sure, Mace."

"Turn on the battery switch and run out about sixty feet of winch cable."

He circled around to the pilot's door and leaned in. Her coat was draped over the back of the pilot's seat and, though it felt oddly voyeuristic, he couldn't resist leaning in to smell her on it and brush his hand down the sleeve.

He flipped the switch then pressed the Down button on the winch control. He laid out the cable on the ground as it unspooled.

"What do you need this for?"

"To get you to where you need to be as soon as I get this bird up and running."

Tim looked up at the smoke plume now streaming thickly over the valley. The first curl of smoke slid down into the valley, smelling warm and homey like walking down Parisian Way along a frozen Larch Creek on a cold Arctic night and smelling the wood smoke from everyone's chimneys.

And then the next curl of smoke brought the scent of burning brush, leaves, and the sharp bite of sap fired off like a million firecrackers and scorching the air.

The Sherpa C-23 returned with its twin plane close behind. Small black dots separated from the plane and parachutes bloomed into being across the smoky sky. He counted five sticks of jumpers and two pallets of gear out of each plane. Twenty smokies and their gear.

"Tell me you're close, Mace. Tell me you're real close."

In answer, she began tossing down tools as fast as he could catch them and chuck them into the box. She pulled out a flashlight and shone it around.

"Nothing left behind?"

"That's what I'm checking, numbskull." She tossed down the grease tube, then waved an open hand at him. "Come on, Tim. I need the engine cowling."

He grabbed the big piece of sheet metal and tried not to scream in frustration while she drove in screws around the edges with a small electric driver.

"Catch me!" And she slid down the side of the LongRanger nowhere near him and landed feet first on the rocky bank of the stream. "Some boyfriend you are. You were supposed to catch me." And she was gone even faster than her teasing smile.

She circled the helo quickly doing a safety check before slipping into the pilot's seat.

Tim had snapped a lifting collar to the hook at the end of the winch line. It was a simple padded donut never used for rescuing an untrained civilian, because they couldn't be trusted. But by putting his head and arms through, then lowering his arms, he was anchored solidly in place for a lift.

"Hope to god this works," Macy muttered as she began cranking the engine.

"I heard that."

"You weren't supposed to, boyfriend."

"Heard that too. Is that what I am?" The two-bladed rotor began to lumber its way around in a circle. Ten seconds for the first blade to go by, five for the second, then two for the first one again.

"Until you put a ring on my finger, boyfriend is as high as it goes." Then she turned to look at him aghast. "I didn't just say that."

The blades kept accelerating.

"Odd," Tim said. "You didn't say it, but I seem to have heard it anyway."

The turboshaft began to wind up in an increasing cry.

"Tell me you weren't thinking it. Please tell me you weren't. That's way too big." Macy had to raise her voice to be heard, but the pleading was still clear.

"Not until your father said it."

"Dad?" She practically whimpered.

The engine settled into its groove, the rotors whipping around at full speed just a yard over his head.

Tim leaned in, took her face in both his hands, and shouted, "How about until after the fire we both agree that we never heard a thing?"

She nodded.

He kissed her quickly. And while she might be beautiful, she was also undeniably cute sitting in a million-dollar machine with a look like she'd just been thrown in the deep end of the pool and had no idea why.

"I'll be back as fast as I can to help," she raised her voice.

"Pick up the hunters first."

She flinched at not thinking about them, "Where is the fire in relation to them?"

"Just go find the point of origin."

"Oh shit!"

Tim nodded, "Your dad should have Vince waiting for you at the hangars when you get your bucket." He could see by her look that he didn't have to say anything else. He backed off, closed the door, and waved her aloft.

Vince had been the town cop ever since Vince's dad had retired. The town had only needed one, so Vince had worked Fairbanks Police Department as a younger man. A Harrison had been the cop of Larch Creek for over sixty years and it was a deep disappointment to Vince that his only son Brett had gone into construction instead. Still, maybe Brett would take over his family's legacy some day.

Vince would take the hunters off Macy's hands. Hopefully Macy wouldn't say anything about point-of-origin for the fire until after she'd delivered them.

Whether it was a runaway campfire or, more likely, exploding targets as they zeroed their rifle scopes, there was little question as to who would be paying for this fire. It was going to be a very expensive trip to Alaska for these Lower Forty-eighters. If they also caught a bonus of the rough edge of Macy Tyler's tongue, then it was no more than they deserved.

She did a few final checks and then began climbing up into the air, slowly finding her way out of the tight space down in the narrow valley.

Tim still didn't know how she'd landed there. That had to have been eight kinds of ugly. Well, the departure would be smoother. He made sure that the winch line took up cleanly with no snarls or snags as she rose.

The last of the slack came out of the winch line and Tim was swept smoothly off his feet.

Macy eased him aloft until he was level with the ridge and then slipped sideways. In a minute he was standing beside Hank, had ducked out of the lifting collar, and waved Macy off. With a side-to-side waggle of the helo she was gone and he turned to face the fire.

The blaze was still a long way off, but it was already chewing over the far edge of the next valley past the one Macy had come down in. If they didn't stop it here, their next chance was another five miles and ten thousand acres to the east. After that, their backs would be against Larch Creek and that wasn't going to happen.

"So what's the plan?" he asked Hank.

Hank looked uncomfortable as he helped Tim put on his harness with his food bag, fire shelter, maps, compass, and a dozen other tools of the trade.

"Where's Tony? Didn't he surface?" It was a common enough occurrence in Alaska for someone to simply leave without telling anyone, but not common for a smokie.

"He surfaced," Hank looked away and then back. "They found him a half mile from his truck. He'd gone back-country after a moose on his day off. Instead he found a bear, or other way around, it found him. Tony downed it point blank with a .45 in the ear while the bear was ripping off his leg at the knee. Applied his own tourniquet and was crawling back out when they found him. They had to take the leg at the thigh. That's why we were slow to respond; most of us were over to the hospital to tease him about all the meat he'd left behind for the wolves by not dragging the bear back with him."

"Oh man," it happened, but...*oh man.*

"So it's you or me, buddy? Toss a coin or are you going to man up after telling the whole damn county that you love Macy?" Hank stuck his thumbs in his harness and rocked back on his heels, very pleased at how smoothly he'd worked in the dig.

Didn't leave Tim a whole lot of choice. But Hank wasn't going to carry the ball into the end zone so easily.

"Okay, *buddy.*"

Hank winced because he could guess well enough that he'd just earned whatever was coming.

"Lead a six-man team to the north. Cut a downslope forty-five, we need to narrow the path on this beast as it climbs the ridge toward us."

It was about the worst cut there was. You had to fell all of the trees uphill rather than the more natural downhill. And then after you trimmed off all of the branches and nipped the heavier undergrowth, you had to drag all the waste upslope as well. The idea was deny fuel to the fire, not add to it.

"Shee-it!" Hank moaned, then started calling for the crew without further hesitation.

Tim turned to face the harder task, figuring out how to make sure this whole team came out of this one safe and sound. Too many of them had a woman or man to get back to.

"Ha!" he barked out the laugh aloud.

A whole lot of them had someone waiting...including him.

CHAPTER 15

*M*acy gathered up the hunters without shooting any of them. One, because she was outnumbered and two, firing her Henry .45-70 always hurt her shoulder. If a grizzly was coming—which is why she carried the big gun aboard her helo—she wouldn't let it stop her. But these hunters...it seemed a waste of effort. Still, they made a tempting target.

They clearly knew what they'd done. Rather than setting up camp or going tracking, they were all sitting on a log near where she'd dropped them off. Only two of them tried pretending nothing was wrong, though they cut it out when she flew close along the edge of the fire. Silence soon reigned supreme in the LongRanger's passenger cabin.

As she passed the leading edge of the fire, Anne Marie's SEAT plane showed up and dumped its first load on the fire. Eight hundred gallons looked like little more than a thimbleful against a backdrop of five hundred acres of blazing trees and flames shooting fifty feet above the treetops.

As she headed down into Larch Creek and saw that Vince was indeed waiting, she spoke on the intercom for the first time in the flight.

"I'm sorry to drop you here rather than back at the airport in Fairbanks, but I'm due back on the fire as fast as possible. Alternate transportation has been arranged."

And just in case Vince couldn't fit them all in his Jeep Grand Cherokee—the only red vehicle in town—there were any number of irate townsfolk gathered at the hangars to watch the show who would be only too glad to escort them to the town's lockup in the basement of the library until they could be transferred to the Fairbanks PD.

She left it for Vince to get them out of her helicopter while she crossed to the hangar to dig out the Bambi bucket and put on her Nomex protective gear in case she went down again and ended up near the flames.

Her father was waiting for her just inside the hangar.

Macy didn't think, she didn't ask. She simply walked straight into his arms and laid her head on his shoulder.

Since the moment the linkage had failed, Macy had held it all together.

Her hands had been steady through Tim announcing to the whole world that he loved her, and her own equally surprising statement to him. She'd focused through delivering the man she loved to fight the fire and retrieving the idiots who had started it.

Macy had been clean on the controls when her engine had cut out, managed to clear the death-dealing ridge by less than ten feet, and found a hole in the trees. With her throttle controls gone it had come down to pitch, roll, and yaw with no spare time for prayer as she autorotated down into the rocky divide. There hadn't even been a moment to radio, either she'd be dead or she could call later.

She'd survived and buried herself in the repair.

But now, safe in her father's arms, the shakes took her until her bones seemed to rattle together.

"God, Daddy. That was so close. So close."

"Knew that when I saw where you were," he patted her back and she noted that his voice wasn't much steadier than her own.

She breathed him in and found comfort. But at the same time she

knew that she'd find even more comfort and just as much under-
standing in Tim's arms.

Most men would be angry or overprotective or something. "A
woman shouldn't be..." "How could you..."

Tim knew what her certifications meant. He knew what it meant
to live in Alaska. And he knew that danger was a part of the job.

"I've got to get going," she pushed away from her dad's chest and
wiped at her eyes.

"You want me to ride along?"

She knew her father didn't like helicopters. Something about the
motion made him queasy in a way that even aerobatics in his biplane
didn't.

"No. I'm okay. Let's get this bucket out. I need to top off the fuel
and get to the fire. There's a man out there that I really need to talk to,
but first I have to go save his ass."

"That's my gal," he grabbed the other end of the Bambi bucket and
they carried it back out into the sunshine.

Two of the hunters were standing by Vince's Jeep. The other two
were on the ground with their hands cuffed behind them.

Vince strolled over to get the rest of their gear out of the back of
her helicopter.

"Seems those two didn't like the idea that they might be liable for a
couple hundred thousand in fire suppression costs alone."

"You're looking awfully pleased there, Vince."

"Suppose I am. Haven't had an excuse to use my cuffs since Claude
Moreau made such a fuss over the Tour de France results a couple
weeks ago and I had to lock him up on a drunk and disorderly until
he dried out. Haven't used them on a real criminal since—"

Macy didn't want to be rude, but she tuned him out and crawled
under her helo to snap the Bambi bucket harness onto the center
cargo hook.

Vince found being the only cop around was a lonely occupation,
and was likely to spin stories out for an hour if you didn't stop him.
Thankfully, he never seemed to take offense when you went about
your business in the middle of his telling one.

She also plugged in the wiring harness that would let her control the bucket's release valve from her cockpit.

When she crawled back out, Vince was still there. Moving with a deliberate slowness as he gathered the hunters' rifles and gear from the passenger cabin, which wasn't like him.

She stood still to show she was listening. A quick look around showed that she could afford a moment. Her father was straightening out the hundred feet of the bucket's lines on the ground so that it would lift cleanly. Tinka had brought over the immaculate 1958 Ford pickup—perhaps the original blue truck of Larch Creek, which matched Tinka's hair and the leather vest that attempted to encircle her generous frame today—with the five-hundred gallon fuel tank on the back and was filling the LongRanger's fuel tanks.

"I couldn't help overhearing…" Vince seemed unusually cautious.

"Overhearing…what?" Macy didn't have a clue.

"Maybe Tim shouldn't have used the general frequency when he said…"

"Oh shit! He didn't!" But she thought back and he had. "I'm going to have to kill him. I know it's a lousy way to start a relationship, but I'm going to have to kill him. Please Vince. Don't arrest me until after I've done the deed."

"Sure, Macy. Whatever you say. I was just wondering about my boy. He…ah…" Even Vince, the king of words in town, at least spoken ones, seemed to be at a loss.

Macy blinked a few times trying to make the connection. His boy…

Vince arranged and rearranged the hunters' four long rifles on the deck of her helo's passenger cabin.

"Oh," she finally got it. His boy Brett. Who she'd had a date with just a few nights ago. Back before Tim had apparently declared to the entire world that he loved her. "Did you hear that Linda Lee is moving back from Talkeetna?"

Vince looked interested, "Can't say as I had."

"Called me last week. I'm going to fly over and bring her back as soon as the divorce is final."

"Seem to remember that she was sweet on Brett, but the boy was a little slow to notice."

"Seem to recall that myself," Macy did her best to match Vince's dry tone.

"Huh," was Vince's comment.

"Might have mentioned that to Brett the other night."

"Really?" Vince considered the thought.

Macy nodded in reply

They stood quietly in silent accord for few moments and then Vince moved smoothly back into action and hefted the rifles. "Some pretty nice equipment here. I see custom work on two of them. Might just have to impound these, pending investigation and all."

"You just might," Macy agreed as Vince offered her a nod and moved off with them. Men were still bizarre, even after they were married and had grown kids. That didn't bode well for Tim. She already didn't understand him. What was going to happen to him in another dozen years or two?

Shit! Why did her thoughts keeping asking questions like that?

Once everyone was clear, Macy lifted back into the sky, doing her best to ignore the several dozen town members who had gathered to watch the show.

Her father blew her a kiss and rested his hand on his heart.

As she looked down at the crowd standing around the *Aéroport d'Orly*, she noticed an inordinate number of them had handheld radios with them. Typical in winter, but not so usual in summer.

Macy would make sure any future declarations between her and Tim happened strictly face to face.

CHAPTER 16

im was barely aware when Macy checked in.

She asked where he wanted a load of water and he directed her. The cascade of white foam that washed down over the edge of the fire was a wonderful surprise that garnered his full attention.

Water usually fell from a Bambi bucket in a blue-white shower that always seemed to cover far too little of the fire. Macy had obviously sprung for the foam attachment that injected a foaming agent into the water. Suddenly two hundred gallons of water acted like two thousand and splattered against the fire in a white shroud.

"That's it, Mace. Work that line and work it hard."

He watched for her next drop, just six minutes later. That meant she'd found a lake or river nearby to hover over and dip her bucket for a reload.

Tim had watched a thousand drops from the ground. Maybe ten thousand. Emily, Jeannie, and the rest of the crew did it for a living, Macy did it as a sideline. She was a good pilot, but probably flew a half dozen fires in a whole season.

"Hold…" he called on her next run. She'd been dropping early. "Now! Drop. Drop. Drop!"

Half a second later a wall of white foam hit the edge of the fire that was threatening to scoot around the edge of Hank's firebreak. With a whorl of smoke, the flames retreated for the moment.

He kept quiet for the next one, but she was better. Not perfect, but he could see her taking the lesson in.

"You weren't compensating for the wind. Next time come in fifty feet higher. You're dropping at the right height for water, but a little low for foam."

He wondered at how easily she took instruction. No ego on the line, just doing it right. Damn but he loved that woman.

That was a problem he'd have to chew on later.

In one of those timeless blinks that happened on a fire, she called that she was headed back to refuel.

Tim had been working the line, spending a little time with each smokie, checking technique—which was generally very solid, Tony had been a good leader—and learning each one's name and strengths.

"Pee and eat while you're down," he told her as he dragged spruce branches Tina had just sliced off a fallen tree. She'd been good with a saw on the Arctic Village fire. But he'd taken to showing her some new tricks and she was really tacking it down.

"Yes, dear," Macy called down as she turned back to Larch Creek.

Yes dear? Like they were already a married couple.

Tim went to drag the next couple branches, which were too big.

"Tina. I'm not Hercules. Fix it," he yelled out over the sound of her saw.

"Says you!" She came over to chop them in half where he indicated. "Seven impossible tasks. Filled Tony's shoes better than Tony could. Made Macy Tyler fall in love with him. That's two down. You're on a roll."

She hit the throttle on the saw cutting off all conversation.

After the cuts were done, she sliced off his ability to respond with additional sharp bursts on the throttle before sneering at him.

"Show me Number Three and maybe I'll consider being impressed," she gunned the throttle once more and turned back to the tree.

Tim grabbed the branches and dragged them off.

Dear? If there was going to be a third miracle it was actually finding some time with Macy.

No. They'd find that as soon as they beat this fire.

It was after that, solving what they were going to do about *"dear."* That would be the true miracle.

Akbar and Laura worked only a few dozen miles apart. They were still trying to solve what to do this winter when MHA took the next Australian contract, but somehow Tim knew they'd work it out.

They'd had time to work it out…he had a week. Actually, he now had only a few days.

And a faceful of smoke reminded him of what he was supposed to be working on.

Macy was back, then gone, then back.

The fire fought, spit, jumped the line, and was beaten back.

Usually night ended drop operations for most pilots. But this close to the Arctic Circle, the hours were long and…

He checked his watch. It was past midnight.

The helicopter and SEAT both soared by close overhead. As the fire had progressed, Macy and Anne Marie had needed less and less instruction. Finally, he'd been able to provide only vague directions and then forget about them. They coordinated between themselves very effectively.

"Air attack, you need to get out of the sky. Don't want to see your faces a minute before eight hours from now."

Anne Marie bitched and groused, but Macy didn't say a word. She simply turned for home without so much as a waggle of her rotors.

It was okay to push yourself on the ground. If he fell down, he could stand back up. If Macy had a moment of inattention and snagged a tree with her bucket, she would be out of the air in a handful of seconds.

He turned back to the fire.

Eight hours later, Macy returned to an entirely different scene than the one she'd left. The fire had burned all of the fuel behind it, leaving a scorched swath across the Alaskan wilderness. It was as if a bucket of black had been dumped from where she'd dropped off the hunters yesterday morning to the ridge guarding the valley where she'd gone down.

But the smokejumpers' firebreak had held.

There were two new gashes through the trees where they had cut fresh breaks while she'd slept in the back of her chopper at the hangar. They had done their jobs and the fire hadn't broken free.

Instead of yesterday's mind-numbing battle against towering flames, she and Anne Marie wandered about the sky for an hour dousing hotspots and flareups.

Smokejumpers wandered through the Black looking like lost souls, as they too hunted and killed hotspots.

By ten o'clock, she began ferrying them out in batches of five with a sling of equipment dangling on a longline below. She delivered them, each and every one, out to the road in front of the *Aéroport d'Orly* where a truck waited to ferry them off.

The last load had only four to carry out.

Tim wasn't there.

"Hank?" she asked carefully, doing her best to not feel afraid. Hank was in the last load.

"He said you'd know where to find him. Something about washing up in a stream." The relief was a cold splash of refreshing water.

When Macy delivered the last of the firefighters to the hangars at Larch Creek, she fetched a half dozen blankets and checked to make sure that Tim's civilian clothes were still in the rear baggage compartment.

She wasn't filthy, but she felt that way; she added soap and a couple towels to her load and headed back to the little valley just past where they had stopped the fire.

CHAPTER 17

im watched Macy circle down into the valley. The LongRanger floated down into the valley as if it was as light as dandelion fluff despite the close canyon walls. Having done it the first time without power, this must have felt easy no matter how unnerving it was to watch.

She didn't look at him as she powered down the helo.

He lay on the bank, still in his full gear, watching her neat, precise movements as the rotor blade wound down from pound, through beat, down to a soft *whoop-whoop,* then stilled into silence.

His ears rang.

Slowly the sounds reemerged, the splashing of the rocky creek, the rustle of the trees in the warm wind that was taking a midday stroll along the valley floor.

Macy stepped down and took his breath away. He'd figured out some things, but he had to see what she was thinking before he dumped them on her.

"You're filthy," she tossed a bar of soap on his chest and a towel beside him.

"You look something of a mess yourself."

"A mess, huh?" she fisted hands on those nice sleek hips of hers.

"Complete and total, Tyler."

She huffed out an angry breath apparently expecting a different conversation. Well, he'd give her that as well.

"How did you get so beautiful and I never noticed?"

"Aw, shucks, Harada. You sure know how to sweet talk a girl."

"Maybe it's that I love you."

At that she dropped down to sit on his nice clean towel.

"What?" he reached out and rested a hand on her knee.

"How am I supposed to work up a good mad when you say something like that?" The tears came so quickly, they caught him struggling upright. She leaned against his shoulder, then pushed him away.

"Faugh! You stink, Tim." She now had a black smear on her forehead. It made him want to wet his forefinger and doodle there.

Instead, he peeled off the smokejumper gear. Layer after layer into a pile.

"I brought you fresh clothes."

That was good because while the air was warm, the valley walls would be blocking the sun soon and he already knew that the stream was icy cold.

He peeled down past the long johns.

"Leave those on," she waved a finger at his underwear and t-shirt. "I won't be able to think if you take those off. Maybe later."

He held out his hands to her, "I only stink of me now, not fire."

She leaned in and sniffed his shoulder, "Not much better."

Then she folded up against him and he pulled her into his lap.

"One day, Tim. All we get is one more day?" it was practically a wail.

"I've been thinking about that, sitting here by this stream waiting for you."

She quieted a bit. He could feel her listening.

"You're a damn good pilot, Mace. MHA likes exceptional pilots; they'd hire you in a heartbeat."

He ignored the way she stiffened and tried to push away, but it wasn't hard to hold her.

"But," he stopped her. "You'd die away from this place. Interior Alaska is a part of your blood."

She held still for a moment, and then gave a resigned nod against his shoulder.

"You heard about, Tony."

She cringed.

"Yeah, I know. But they want to offer me his job, lead jumper."

That bolted her upright. He'd been nuzzling her hair and she cracked her head against his nose hard enough that he saw nothing but stars and shooting lights of pain for a moment.

"God dabbit, Bace," he sounded like a clown as he pinched the bridge of his nose.

"I warned you," she managed in a gasp. She started to giggle, fought it, failed, fought it again and then totally collapsed into the grass beside him. Tears of laughter were streaming down her face. Tears that started shifting toward hysteria.

At a total loss of what to do with the shockwaves of Macy's emotions, Tim finally leaned down and kissed her. In an instant she calmed and lay there looking up at him with those wide brown eyes.

"What did you say to them? Are you going to take the job?"

"That's up to you."

"No. No. No!" She sat back up and waved both her hands at him palm out in a stopping motion.

He raised a hand to protect his nose just in case.

"You are not putting this one on me. You have to do what's right for you and not—"

"Shut up, Tyler."

Much to his surprise, she did.

"The job doesn't depend on you."

"Okay then."

"Whether or not I take it depends on if we're getting married and I'm moving back to Larch Creek."

MACY KNEW there were times when stunned amazement or panic weren't called for. Like when she'd been trying to land her Long-Ranger right here with a dead stick.

And those were the moments where hesitation didn't work, only immediate action sufficed.

She dove on Tim, driving him back to prone, and kissed him. Hard. Rubbed her nose against his.

He winced and twitched and swore—no doubt that's what he was doing despite the kiss. He finally managed to mumble, "Carbul of by dose."

She kissed the tip of it for good measure.

"I take it that's a yes."

Macy sat on his chest and looked down at him. She wasn't going to let him go anywhere. It was a *HUGE* yes. But...

"What about Akbar and MHA? You've talked about him so much I feel as if I know him better than you."

"No one knows me better than you, Mace."

"Maybe once but—"

"No. Still. Akbar changed when he met Laura. His outsides still think he's all bravado and ever so cool, but inside he's so sweet on her. It confused the hell out of me, but now I understand. I know that feeling Mace. It's this." He reached up one of those big hands of his and cupped the side of her face. That it smelled of smoke and woods and hot leather gloves didn't matter. It was Tim.

"So, you'd trade that in to be lead smokejumper here?"

"I liked it. I liked discovering that I knew fire just as well as Akbar the Great. We beat that thing, Mace. You, me, Hank, the others. We did that and I wouldn't take credit away from any of them. But I can tell you: it was a fantastic high to take the lead. I know that I'm the one who really beat that sucker; both of them actually, here and Arctic Village."

His smile was the twelve-year-old boy, the moment before she'd chased him around the yard with a two-by-four. It was the fourteen-year old who had dragged her into his mother's Kung Fu classes. And the eighteen-year old as she'd stood between him and Stephen on the senior prom night.

"But it's a short fire season up here, isn't it?" She knew full well it was. She didn't know why she was arguing. Macy wanted Tim to be here so badly, but she didn't want him waking up a year or two from now and cursing the trap she'd placed him in either.

"That's the part I'm not so sure about," Tim's eyes drifted skyward, then down the valley toward Denali. "I'm sure I could stay on with MHA for the off-season work, Australia or wherever, but then I'd be gone for six months a year."

"We could do that…" though she didn't know how. But if she had to live through the dark winters alone in order to have Tim half the year, she'd do it.

"I know. It's not the right answer, but it's the best I found so far. Heck, Mace. Macy. My lovely Macy Tyler. I don't want to be away from you a single night, never mind six months every year. It's not that you're dragging me back to Alaska. I feel like I'm home here. That's something I lost in the Lower Forty-eight. I want to be here, with you."

No longer using her childhood nickname for distance, now it was as if he was sweeping her in. If he hadn't already made a marriage proposal, that would have been a good one.

"I was hoping you had a better idea."

"Me?" her voice squeaked.

"Yeah, you, pretty lady." Then he reached up and began unbuttoning her shirt.

She looked at him askance. Slapping at his hands had no effect.

"It doesn't seem right that I'm the only person in this valley wearing nothing but their underwear."

"Me." Like that made even the least bit of sense. She did her best to ignore him as he continued undressing her.

There was an idea.

An idea tickling away in the back of her head.

He released her bra and then traced her breast with that rough, powerful, gentle hand of his.

As she leaned into it, she pictured a pile of manuscripts stacked in his mother's office.

Real potential, Eva had said. *Loved writing but didn't have enough time.*

Tim had forgotten about that dream.

He leaned down and kissed her breast and she wrapped her arms around his smoky hair and held onto him.

It was easy to picture Tim fighting fires in the summer…

He lay her onto her back and now she was the one looking up at the blue sky.

…writing in the winter…

Then he finished undressing them both and lay down upon her.

…and coming home to her every night.

She wrapped her arms around the dream come to life that even holding Tim sent washing over her.

Her solution could wait for later. Because she finally knew that they were going to have a whole lot of laters.

TO KEEP BURNING UP THE PAGES IN THIS SERIES, READ:

(EXCERPT)

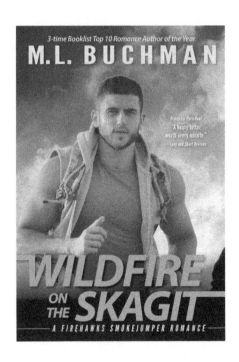

WILDFIRE ON THE SKAGIT
(EXCERPT)

"*Guard your reserves!*" *The* spotter shouted after he'd clambered from the cockpit, over all of the smokejumpers, and finally reached the back door of the roaring DC-3 jump plane.

Krista Thorson slapped her hand over her reserve parachute to make sure it didn't accidentally deploy when he popped open the door. A glance down the line assured her that all twelve smoke-jumpers in the flight were awake and doing the same.

A DC-3's cabin wasn't that cramped, until you piled wildland fire-fighting gear secure behind heavy cargo nets down one side, and a dozen fully geared up smokejumpers prone like beached whales down the other. They'd been trying to finish their night's sleep after the dawn call-to-fire, but the wildfire was so close to base that a catnap was all any of them had gotten.

Krista and Akbar "the Great" Jepps, the lead smokie, were always first stick. It had taken Krista a decade to work up to the Number Two slot. When Tim and before him TJ had still been on the crew, she was rarely out of the plane in the first pass—two jumpers was a typical stick for each passage of the plane over a jump spot.

It was a good, comfortable slot. Despite her constant threats to drop a tree on him and take over, she really wasn't interested in Lead; Akbar was just too damned good and she couldn't imagine jumping with anyone else.

Being Number Two in the first stick also meant that she got to test the air first, find a way down through the roaring winds so chaotic near a fire. She loved the challenge.

Fifteen minutes out from the fire they'd safety-checked each others' gear, from heavy jumpsuit pants secured at the boots so no tree branch could slip by, to parachute harness, to helmet with wire-mesh face mask. They were as ready as they could be.

Terry, Mount Hood Aviation's spotter for *Jump M1*, popped the rear door and pulled it inward. There was a slap of wind, especially where she and Akbar sat crammed at the rear of the plane—just the sort of slap that could snag a reserve parachute, then suck it and the attached smokie out the door after straining her through the metal hull.

Through the open door the smell of high mountain air and hot engine exhaust swirled about the cabin. The DC-3's big radial engines were no longer buffered by the airplane's thin hull, but now delivered their full-throated roar right into the open jump door—sweet music of the first jump of the fire season.

"Did you remember to call her this time?" Krista leaned down and shouted at Akbar. He was powerfully muscled, and over half a foot shorter than Krista's six feet plus. He was India's answer to Tom Cruise, except he was younger, fitter, and from Seattle. But just as short, which she'd usually remind him about now, but he was looking all freaked out.

"Crap!" He yanked out his cell phone as Krista laughed. He never remembered to warn his wife he was about to jump a fire and might not be able to call for days.

"You'd be lost without me, dude!"

"I'd be more lost without her," he shouted back.

Amazing, but true.

Akbar the Great had always been a rocking firefighter—there was a reason he was the lead smokie with such an elite outfit. He'd also been the crassest of womanizers. Right until the moment he met Laura Jenson. She'd done something to him, and not just stopping his ever-growing circle of post-fire flings.

He wasn't any less aggressive against a burn, but he was—

Krista searched for the right word.

—steadier?

Whatever it was, Laura had definitely been a good influence on Akbar. And on top of making Akbar behave, she was also a wilderness guide and expert horsewoman which made her real easy to respect. The fact that she was a totally likeable person just meant Akbar was way luckier than he deserved.

If he was a little less freaking happy all the time, he might be more tolerable. Of course, he was getting it regular from a wonderful woman, so maybe he had reason to be so goofy happy that Krista wanted to smack him sometimes.

Often.

What the hell. She smacked his shoulder hard.

"What was that for?" he shouted as he huddled over his phone.

"Just 'cause."

There was no way for Akbar to call now, not over the roar of engine and hundred mile-an-hour wind ripping by the door, so he sent a quick text Krista could see over his shoulder.

Fire.

"C'mon, dude. You been married a year and you still don't know shit." After a year—hell, Laura was a smart woman—after the first twenty minutes, she must have known what sort of a man Akbar was. Didn't mean that Krista couldn't tease him about it anyway.

"What?"

"You gotta tell her you love her or something. Most girls want to hear stuff like that."

He nodded about six times as if trying to embed that in his memory, but she knew it wouldn't stick.

"Now!"

"Oh, right." He scrambled out a quick "Hugs" on his phone and looked pretty pleased with himself. Sad.

Then he glanced up at her, as he stuffed away his phone. "Not you, though. I forget that Mama Krista is not like other girls."

Krista shrugged. All that romantic, mushy stuff had never done much for her. Still, if she hadn't learned to ignore that specific phrase from hearing it so many times that she was immune to it—mostly— she'd consider sending Akbar down without his parachute.

Not like other girls. She was too goddamn tall, broad-shouldered enough that guys (at least the ones with a death wish) asked if she played front four on the football team, and she was stronger than any of them. *Not like other girls,* had plagued her since birth. If she—

Krista shoved her growing anger aside, pissed that it had slid up around her guard—again.

available at fine retailers everywhere

ABOUT THE AUTHOR

M.L. Buchman started the first of, what is now over 50 novels and even more short stories, while flying from South Korea to ride his bicycle across the Australian Outback. All part of a solo around-the-world bicycle trip (a mid-life crisis on wheels) that ultimately launched his writing career.

Booklist has selected his military and firefighter series(es) as 3-time "Top 10 Romance of the Year." NPR and Barnes & Noble have named other titles "Best 5 Romance of the Year." In 2016 he was a finalist for RWA's prestigious RITA award.

He has flown and jumped out of airplanes, can single-hand a fifty-foot sailboat, and has designed and built two houses. In between writing, he also quilts. M. L. is constantly amazed at what you can do with a degree in Geophysics. He also writes: contemporary romance, thrillers, and fantasy.

More info and a free novel for subscribing to his newsletter at: www.mlbuchman.com

Join the conversation:
www.mlbuchman.com

Other works by M. L. Buchman:

SIGN UP FOR M. L. BUCHMAN'S NEWSLETTER TODAY

and receive:
Release News
Free Short Stories
a Free novel

Do it today. Do it now.
www.mlbuchman.com/newsletter

CPSIA information can be obtained
at www.ICGtesting.com
Printed in the USA
FSHW021909081019
62814FS